Cathy Williams

CLAIMING HIS CINDERELLA SECRETARY

HARLEQUIN® PRESENTS®

Recycling programs for this product may not exist in your area.

ISBN-13: 978-1-335-56885-4

Claiming His Cinderella Secretary

This edition published by arrangement with Harlequin Books S.A.

For questions and comments about the quality of this book, please contact us at CustomerService@Harlequin.com.

Harlequin Enterprises ULC
22 Adelaide St. West, 40th Floor
Toronto, Ontario M5H 4E3, Canada
www.Harlequin.com

Printed in U.S.A.

Ellie thought of the prim and proper clothes she had dragged along with her.

She breathed a sigh of relief that she'd had the chance to blow some of her money on a couple of things that would make a better impression in the casual tropical setting she had not given sufficient thought to when she had flung open the doors of her wardrobe in London. For three years, surrounded by her brainy, wild and wacky colleagues, she had stuck rigidly to the background persona she had molded herself into. Years of anxiety, years of looking after her mother, years of sublimating her own grief in the face of bigger concerns, had conferred a serious maturity on young shoulders.

Here, though...under these hot, turquoise skies and velvet, starry nights, she would stop being that careful young woman, risk averse and taking no chances.

So her boss thought she was Little Miss Efficient and Ever So Slightly Dull?

Well, wouldn't it give her a kick to prove to James that there was a bit more to her than knee-length skirts and sensible shoes...

Secrets of the Stowe Family

Their next destination? True love!

When Max, Izzy and James's parents died in a tragic accident, all they had left was each other… Max, the oldest Stowe sibling, had to take charge, bring up his brother and sister—*and* take the helm of the family business.

Years later, their family business has been transformed into a global success! Still, there's more to life than just work, isn't there? It's time for the Stowe siblings to discover, as they travel the world, the business of love!

Meet the Stowe family in…

Max and Mia's story
Forbidden Hawaiian Nights

Izzy and Gabriel's story
Promoted to the Italian's Fiancée

James and Ellie's story
Claiming His Cinderella Secretary

All available now!

Cathy Williams can remember reading Harlequin books as a teenager, and now that she is writing them, she remains an avid fan. For her, there is nothing like creating romantic stories and engaging plots, and each and every book is a new adventure. Cathy lives in London, and her three daughters—Charlotte, Olivia and Emma—have always been, and continue to be, the greatest inspirations in her life.

Books by Cathy Williams

Harlequin Presents

The Tycoon's Ultimate Conquest
Contracted for the Spaniard's Heir
Marriage Bargain with His Innocent
The Italian's Christmas Proposition
His Secretary's Nine-Month Notice
The Forbidden Cabrera Brother

Conveniently Wed!

Shock Marriage for the Powerful Spaniard

Once Upon a Temptation

Expecting His Billion-Dollar Scandal

Secrets of the Stowe Family

Forbidden Hawaiian Nights
Promoted to the Italian's Fiancée

Visit the Author Profile page
at Harlequin.com for more titles.

CHAPTER ONE

WHERE IN GOD'S name was she?

James pushed his chair back, swivelled it at an angle so that he could relax back, feet up on his desk, folded his hands behind his head and scowled darkly at his office door, which had been slammed shut just a few minutes ago.

Actually, *slammed* risked being an understatement. He was surprised the thing was still on its hinges. Naomi, his now ex-girlfriend, had stormed out of his office, blazingly angry, only just managing to resist the temptation to hurl one of her designer Jimmy Choos at his head.

Her raised voice had been loud enough to shatter glass. Certainly, his entire office must have stopped dead in their tracks. He suspected they might well have downed tools completely so that they could huddle and dissect what they had heard, and doubtless he would be peppered with questions the second he stepped foot out of his office.

There were distinct disadvantages to being a boss with an 'open door, feel free to speak your mind' policy, he decided. A hub filled with young computer geniuses who thrived on the encouragement he gave them to enjoy the informality of his state-of-the-art workspace in order to nurture their creativity had spawned, he glumly thought now, a team of outspoken employees who wouldn't think twice about a formal inquisition into Naomi's noisy departure. Who could resist a full-blown gossip-fest about a woman whose parting shot had been that 'he hadn't heard the last of this'?

Right now, he needed his cool, level-headed secretary to return some semblance of normality to what remained of the day, but where the heck was she in his hour of need?

Next to him, his mobile phone buzzed. He looked at it, saw it was Naomi, and decided that any further conversations would be futile—although he knew she wasn't the type to take things lying down. He had no interest in picking up where they had left off. What more could there be to shout about? And neither was he interested in any kind of reconciliation. The relationship was dead in the water and he had to acknowledge that he had sleepwalked his way into that one.

He'd thought what they had was fun. He'd assumed she was on the same page as him. She'd talked about her career as a catwalk model and how it would be the perfect springboard for her to branch out into fashion design. She'd claimed to be a career woman with no time for anything permanent. She had shown him drawings she had done for a collection of casual wear, and hadn't batted an eyelid when he had accidentally held up the first sketch the wrong way. She'd been the epitome of easy going, so who could have blamed him when he'd casually asked her if she would like to accompany him to his brother's wedding in Hawaii?

They were to spend a few days in the Caribbean, because he'd wanted to seal a deal with a promising start-up company in Barbados. She had been given free rein to choose whatever five-star hotel she wanted, no expense spared. There would be luxury on tap, she would be able to do as she pleased during the day while he worked and they would have the nights to themselves. Of course, he would only get through the preliminaries. Pinning down the final deal would require his trusty PA, so he would have to conclude business in London, but he would have been able to kick-start the process. Then they were to have a leisurely tour of the various Hawaiian islands before the wedding.

It had all made perfect sense and would have

spared him the headache of going to Max's wedding on his own. Personally, he had nothing against people getting married, even though he'd only just recovered from the shock of his die-hard bachelor brother waxing lyrical about the joys of tying the knot.

As a result of his own experiences, however—and from the experiences of some of his friends, who had flung themselves headlong into wedlock at way too young and tender an age, only to regret the impulse a couple of years down the road—commitment and everything it entailed was a game he had no intention of playing any time soon. Hence the prospect of being the best man and bachelor-in-residence at his brother's wedding had filled him with a certain amount of dread. He had been to five weddings in the past six years. And, was it his imagination or were all the unattached females at weddings sprinkled with some kind of weird fairy dust that suddenly made them want to fall in love and rush down the aisle? Having Naomi on his arm, he had concluded, would be the speediest route to making sure he wasn't targeted by anyone with stars in their eyes. Naomi, like him, knew just what relationships were all about. Fun. No strings attached. Just two adults enjoying one another.

Except he'd been wrong.

James snorted at his own idiocy in thinking

that she had been as casual about their affair as he had, but was spared the frustration of dwelling further on the hissy fit to which he had just been subjected by one firm knock followed by the soft push of his office door opening.

'About time.' He swept his feet off the desk and briskly sat forward as Ellie leaned round to hand him a mug of coffee—strong, sugarless and black. Just the thing he needed. The woman was a mind reader.

'About time?'

Ellie looked at her charismatic, wildly sexy boss and suppressed the usual shiver of unwelcome awareness that rippled through her every time she saw him.

She'd been working for James Stowe for three years and he still managed to have an annoying effect on her, although she had always been adept at concealing it under a calm, professional exterior. She wasn't a fool. She knew that an inconvenient attraction was just an annoying blip, easily swatted away, and it was easy enough to swat away because Ellie was sensible enough to conclude that what attracted her was the pull of the opposite. Her stupidly sexy boss was brilliant, utterly unafraid of taking risks and enjoyed the sort of sybaritic, revolving door love life that privately made her shudder. Never mind the more prosaic fact that she'd seen some of the women he dated, and the possibility of him being attracted to her was as far-fetched as a lion being drawn to a mouse.

It was an environment where the dress code was 'anything goes', and the excess energy of the young, talented thirty-strong staff was burnt off at the ping pong table, the darts board or in one of the 'debating rooms', where they could exchange their ideas as forcefully as they wanted. But Ellie always dressed in a uniform of sober suits and flats and, whatever energy she wanted to burn off, she did it at the local swimming pool once a week.

Where her boss was stupidly clever and outspoken in a way that sometimes made her feel faint, Ellie was just the opposite, and she privately maintained that that was the reason why they worked so harmoniously together.

'Where have you been?'

Ellie calmly swerved to sit at the leather chair in front of his desk. She glanced down at her tablet, which she had brought in as she always did, to make notes about whatever mountain of urgent emails he needed her to deal with. When she looked at him, it was to find him glaring at her.

'To the dentist,' she said briskly. Disgruntled

blue eyes met her calm grey ones and she fought not to flush.

He was so beautiful, it was almost a sin. His hair was chestnut-brown, thick and straight. His features were chiselled to perfection, his nose straight, his mouth full of sensuous, wicked promise. Sometimes in the early hours of the morning, when her thoughts were prone to drifting, an image of him would pop into her head and she would savour the taboo pleasure of thinking about the six-foot-two alpha male with the kind of loose limbed, careless grace that made heads turn.

Of course in the cold light of day such thoughts never intruded, and if they did it was easy to dampen them because any woman in the presence of a guy like him could be excused for feeling a bit tingly now and again.

'Did you tell me that you weren't going to be in until…?' he made a show of consulting his Rolex *'…two-thirty in the afternoon?'*

'Of course I did. I also emailed you to remind you a couple of days ago. If you'd like, I can have the email printed off—'

'Not necessary,' James growled, waving down the suggestion dismissively. 'I suppose you've heard what's happened?' He didn't wait for her to answer. 'This office is a hotbed of gossip. It's impossible to have any kind of private life here!

I expect you were grabbed the second you came through that door? Treated to every tiresome detail of the drama that unfolded in your absence? Which, incidentally, would not have happened if you'd been at your desk instead of in a dentist's chair! How's the tooth, anyway?'

'The tooth is fine. Thank you for asking.'

'So…?'

'Trish *did* mention that there was something of…er…an incident with…your girlfriend,' Ellie admitted.

'An incident?'

'It's none of my business,' Ellie said diplomatically in an attempt to divert her boss from the looming onslaught of thunderous rage.

Darling of the gossip pages as he was, and photographed on practically a weekly basis with one of his women glued to his side, he was fiercely protective of his space in the office. Girlfriends were not allowed within the hallowed walls of the converted factory in Shoreditch which housed some of the sharpest computer brains in the country, and their counterparts with business acumen.

Ellie shuddered to think of the reception Naomi would have had, and knew the ensuing drama would have made his blood boil.

His staff all knew that he was a guy who didn't believe in longevity when it came to relationships with women. Although nearly every member of staff felt free to quiz him about whatever latest hot model happened to be gracing his bed, he was actually remarkably tight-lipped when it came to discussing his private life. He threw out just enough by way of answers to satisfy curiosity, but who really knew what motivated a man who seemed so averse to settling down?

Ellie, who never asked questions, wondered whether she was the only one to notice that reticence—the way he never really shared anything meaningful about himself.

Did he do so with anyone?

She realised that she was bursting with curiosity about the blow-up with Naomi but she impatiently put a lid on it. Curiosity about her boss would end up being ruinous for their working relationship, and way too challenging for her peace of mind.

'The whole thing could have been avoided,' he growled, ignoring her lack of input with the sweeping nonchalance of someone accustomed to a rapt audience. 'Naomi should have known better than to show up where I work. I've always made it very clear to the women I date that play is one thing, but work is quite another, and the two don't overlap. Stop staring at that tablet as though it's going to rescue you from sitting here.'

Ellie looked up. 'I thought you wanted the business with Neco Systems sorted at the speed of light in case someone else came along and snapped them up. I spent the morning compiling the contract. I thought we could run through it before I emailed it to you.'

'If you'd been at your desk, you could have escorted her out. Tactfully.'

'It's not my job to deal with your girlfriends, and why would I have escorted her out?'

'Because you know I don't indulge women here unless they work for me.'

Ellie gave up on any prospect of her tablet rescuing her from a conversation she both did and didn't want to have. Somehow indulging in any kind of personal conversation with her boss felt all wrong. It almost felt *threatening*. But what really scared her was the element of *excitement* that went hand in hand with that. He was so clever, so restless, so intrinsically edge-of-seat, addictively commanding.

Part of her wondered what would happen if she allowed herself to be sucked into the vortex of his overpowering personality but somewhere deep inside she had always known that nothing good would come of it.

She didn't want to talk about his women. She wanted to keep things strictly on a polite, harmonious surface level. She didn't want anything confusing to disrupt the calm surface of her life. She'd spent far too many years dealing with chaos and confusion in her own personal life to court yet more of it from another source. She knew that, when it came to James, it would be very easy for the lines between boss and secretary to blur at the edges. He wouldn't notice, but *she* would.

She enjoyed and needed this job. She certainly needed the money and she wasn't about to jeopardise any of that by crossing her own self-imposed boundaries.

'Perhaps you didn't make that clear enough,' Ellie said vaguely.

Naomi had been on the scene for nearly five months, which was something of a record for him. Maybe the poor woman thought that that had constituted the sort of commitment most women sought in a relationship, and therefore that showing up at his workplace wouldn't have resulted in the Spanish Inquisition.

'Of course I made it crystal-clear.' He looked at her with incredulity, as though she'd suddenly started speaking a foreign language, and she returned his gaze coolly, as always. 'Say what you're thinking, Ellie. I can see the cogs whirring, so why don't you spit it out instead of sitting there in fulminating silence?'

Ellie gave up. He could be volatile…energetic in a way that left most people feeling that they were stuck in the slow lane even though they were going as fast as they could. And there were times when she'd had to fade into the background when he had blown a fuse at some hapless person's incompetence.

That said, his moods had always swept past her, leaving her unscathed. He tiptoed around her, respecting the lines between them, and she suspected that, after a string of unsatisfactory secretaries before her, he did his utmost to protect their working relationship. He had curbed his inclination to engage her in discussing her private life. His natural tendency to be provocative and push the barriers had taken a back seat in the face of her quiet resistance.

By nature, Ellie was reserved. It was ironic that she had managed to find herself working in an environment that nurtured exuberance. When it came to recruitment James had chosen carefully, compiling a team of thirty-strong employees who would all coalesce perfectly. Nerdy, yet confident, cutting-edge-clever and not afraid of waging a war to be heard, competitive, yet smart enough to know when to back down. And, of course, however rowdy they became they were all intensely loyal to their brilliant leader. Since she'd been working there, not a single one had come close to quitting.

Amongst this hand-picked crowd, Ellie was the only one who kept herself to herself. She couldn't remember a time when she'd had their free-spirited exuberance. As an only child, she had been loved but cossetted. Her parents had had her late in their lives, after many years of trying for a baby, and she had become the recipient of their reluctance to allow her to do anything that might possibly put her in harm's way.

They had been a unit of three until her father had died when she'd been sixteen, and after that the placid, comfortingly predictable life she had led had come to a crashing halt. Gone were the family days and the quiet holidays to Wales. Gone were the board games in winter and her parents both anxiously waiting up for her to return on the occasional evening out with friends.

Instead, her mother had gone to pieces, and Ellie had had to grow up fast to deal with that. Between the ages of sixteen and twenty, her life had been put on hold. University dreams had been shelved. She had made it through the rest of school, but all her spare time had been taken up saving her mother from herself.

As a couple, her parents had been unbreakable, but when one half of that couple had been removed—in her father's case a mere four months after having been diagnosed with cancer—the structure had catastrophically collapsed. Without Robbie Thompson, her mother had been cast adrift, first retreating into herself and then becoming dependent on alcohol to help herself cope.

Looking back, Ellie marvelled that she had managed to get through school at all, but she had. She had said goodbye to her dream of being an architect, and instead had thrown her energy and talent into absorbing everything there was to know about computer systems. Through it all, she had continued to look after her mother, coaxing her out of her alcohol dependency. They were now at a point where her mother was relatively stable, although after two minor heart attacks she was a shadow of the woman she had once been.

The house had been sold and enough money scraped together to find her somewhere small by the coast, but depression dogged her, and when Ellie thought about it she wanted to burst into tears.

The experience had left her guarded, protective of her privacy and always careful to take nothing for granted. Safety and stability were the two things she craved most because confusion and unpredictability had been terrifying.

Now, James was breaking their unspoken code and was looking at her, eyes bright and challenging, daring her to open up with what she was thinking. She was tempted, because on this one subject she had strong feelings.

'Like I said,' she repeated quietly, 'I don't have any opinions on what you do outside work.'

'Yes, you do.'

Their eyes met and he grinned and visibly relaxed.

'Was there a reason why she came here?' Ellie eventually asked, and he shrugged and nodded to his private sitting area where he entertained clients or had informal meetings—deep leather chairs, a metal table, and to one side a sofa-bed, because it wasn't unheard of for him to spend the night in the office if things were particularly busy.

'Let's go and relax. Been one hell of a day, and we're not even halfway through it. My head's not in a suitable work space.'

'You're the boss,' Ellie said, and he frowned.

'Yes. I am. You work for me, but once in a while it's okay to take off the professional hat and actually stop hiding away behind that glass wall of yours.'

Ellie blushed. She lowered her eyes, but she could feel a tell-tale pulse jumping in her neck. She was keenly aware of him vaulting to his feet, pushing back the leather chair and heading towards the seating area which was brick-walled and warmly inviting.

'And dump the tablet,' he ordered without glancing round at her, making for the sofa-bed, where he proceeded to lie down with his eyes closed. 'Tell me what you're thinking,' he coaxed. 'Get it off your chest. Trust me, you'll feel better for it.'

Ellie was shrewd enough to realise what was happening here. For once, he had found himself in a situation over which he had had no control. Naomi had shown up out of the blue, blown a hole in his day by creating a scene and had left him edgy and in need of venting. The more she tried to pull back, the more he would goad her into a response. For once, she was in the direct line of fire, and the speediest way to return things to normal would be to give up and go with the flow.

'Maybe Naomi thought you wouldn't hit the roof because she made the mistake of showing up here.' Ellie had taken one of the chairs, and she looked at him sprawled out on the sofa-bed, feet loosely crossed at the ankles, eyes now opened to slits as he looked at her, hands folded behind his head. 'You *have* been going out for quite a long time, after all…'

'A handful of months.'

'That's record-breaking for you,' Ellie said politely, driven to honesty, because he just wouldn't let it go. She felt a surge of annoyance that she had been prodded into going against the grain. Rebellion began to blossom inside her, a little voice telling her that, if he wanted to hear what she thought, then why not give him what he wanted?

James grinned and visibly relaxed. 'So it is. You're a tonic, Eleanor Thompson—five-foot six inches, twenty-four years old and a mystery after three years of working for me. How is it that you know how long I've been seeing Naomi, and yet I don't even know whether you have a boyfriend or not? Have you?' He laughed. 'No need to answer that one, Ellie. I already know that your answer will be that it's none of my business, and of course you'd be absolutely right.'

Ellie stiffened. When she looked down, she saw her neat flats, the smooth navy of her knee-length skirt and the white of her ribbed summer tee shirt.

The amusement in his voice ratcheted up that small rebellious voice. Did he imagine that she had no feelings? That she was as dull as dishwater? When he said that she was a *mystery*, it certainly wasn't in the tone of voice that implied she was intriguing.

'It doesn't matter whether you have a list of dos and don'ts when it comes to women,' she told him evenly. 'Most women don't expect to be hauled in front of a firing squad if they make the mistake of paying a visit to the company where their partner works. I know you must have told her what was and wasn't allowed in a relationship but…'

She stopped in mid-flow. Did she really know anything about relationships? Precious little. Fate had made sure to deny her the chance to have fun with guys in the way every other girl her age did. But she did know what she would and wouldn't want in an ideal world, and she definitely wouldn't want any guy who had a book of instructions of what was allowed.

Her heart sped up as their eyes met and she felt a little burst of satisfaction at having said what was in her mind—toning it down, of course, because the lines of demarcation prevented her from really saying what she thought.

What she really thought was that James Stowe was way too clever, way too good-looking and way too charismatic for his own good. In the cut-throat world of computers and computer software, he ruled the roost and now, as he expanded into the lucrative field of tech start-ups, he was on course for claiming the crown.

Women flocked to him because he was the ultimate catch. Except for the fact that he had no sticking power. Just because he made a big deal of laying all his cards on the table at the start of a relationship, didn't mean that he was the epitome of the gentleman, which it seemed was how he would like to be perceived.

'But…?' he encouraged, eyes bright with interest. 'I'm all ears.'

'But women aren't robots,' Ellie said sharply. 'They're not always going to do as you tell them. You're confusing them with people you pay to work for you. They're not employees, and if somewhere along the line they think it might be okay to come here for a surprise visit, then I don't think it's very fair for you to let rip because they've gone against your commands.'

She was huffing a little as he slid off the couch to saunter across to the window, where he stood for a couple of seconds, back to her, peering out.

Energised.

'You make me sound like a tyrant,' he mused, turning round and then strolling towards her. 'Have you always felt that way?'

'I…'

'Yes? Now you've started, you can't leave me hanging on. That would be cruel…'

'You did ask me what I thought.' She inwardly winced at the defensive note in her voice. How had this conversation become so derailed? The devil works on idle hands, she thought. For once his hands had been idle, and in she'd walked, perfectly placed for him to have a little Machiavellian fun at her expense.

He perched on the solid, wooden square table in front of her and leant forward, his forearms on his thighs, his fingers loosely linked.

'And I'm very glad that I did,' he murmured soothingly. 'How else would I have known just how much resentment you were stockpiling for me?'

'I haven't been stockpiling resentment, James!' she cried, dismayed. Her cheeks were hectic with colour and she was leaning towards him, every nerve and pulse in her stretched taut with tension. 'She got the wrong idea.'

'What do you mean? What are you talking about?' Pinned to the spot by incisive blue eyes, Ellie couldn't move a muscle. Her jaw ached from the effort of swallowing and her breathing was shallow and uneven.

Her thoughts were all over the place, because the conversation felt intimate. The gap between them had been breached and she didn't like it.

'Naomi wasn't chucked out of my office. I'm not quite the monster you seem to think I am.'

'I don't think anything of the sort!'

'Sure, she surprised me by coming here and, sure, I don't encourage women to pay impromptu visits to my office. This is where I work. That said, she showed up, and I was perfectly happy to make her a cup of coffee, take time out for fifteen minutes and then escort her out but…'

He shrugged. 'The conversation didn't go as expected. It seems that Naomi equated an invite to Max's wedding with a declaration of intent from me. She showed me pictures of the dress she wanted to wear to the wedding and then she hinted one too many times that she wanted more than fun…that she thought it might be time for me to meet the parents. I thought she was kidding and, when I told her that I thought she understood the score, she went ballistic. Women may not be robots, Ellie, but they should be astute enough to know where I stand on the subject of longevity when I've been upfront with them from the start.'

'Poor Naomi…' Ellie could think of nothing worse than actually falling for someone like James Stowe.

'Poor *Naomi*?'

'Her hopes were raised and you dashed them, and I don't suppose you were all that tactful with it.'

He burst out laughing and she threw him a shadow of a smile.

'And just for your information, James, I'm not at all resentful. I love my job. It's challenging and absorbing and, if I don't happen to agree with how you approach relationships, then that's just a personal thing and I don't want you thinking… I wouldn't want that to somehow…'

'It won't.' He waved down her stumbling apology. He looked at her curiously, head tilted to one side. 'Would *you* have thrown a hissy fit if the guy you were dating told you he wasn't into love and marriage?'

'I wouldn't be dating any guy who wasn't prepared to be serious,' Ellis said bluntly. Once again, she was swamped by a feeling of inappropriate intimacy, although she knew that that was on her part. As far as James was concerned, for once they would simply be conversing as two people instead of as boss and employee. He was casual with all his staff and he encouraged them to talk to him about anything and everything. It was all part of his immense charm.

Six months ago, he had spent an hour holed up with her friend Trish, providing her with a shoulder to cry on because she'd broken up with her boyfriend and was finding it hard to concentrate. He had listened, handed out tissues and then offered her one of his houses abroad for a week's vacation with a friend, all paid for by him.

'That's a tall order for a guy.'

'It's a tall order for *you*.' She flushed and then stood up, smoothing down her skirt.

When their eyes met, she could tell that he was amused and sure enough, his eyebrows raised, barely stifling a grin, he said, 'I see the work hat is back on.'

'There's a lot to get through today.'

'I think we've got through quite a bit already,' James mused softly. 'More than could be expected.'

Ellie flinched. He had managed to slide his foot through the door. Not by much, but enough, and she quailed at the prospect of him thinking that a foot through the door somehow gave him permission to introduce a new level to their well-oiled working relationship.

Ellie knew that she was overreacting. When you worked closely with someone, when you were with them day after day, hour upon hour, it was impossible *not* to let them into your life. The fact that she had held him at bay for so long was the very reason for his curiosity about her.

She wished, somewhere deep inside her, that she could be different…that she could be more open. But she'd always been quiet, and that reserved nature had become something more after her dad had died.

Being responsible for her mother had made her independent. She had had no one to help deal with the loss of the person she loved. Her parents had both been only children and, as she was an only child, there had just been her. Her friends had had their own teenage lives to lead. At first they had been sympathetic, but bit by bit the whole business of living had grabbed their attention and, one by one, they had faded away, occasionally glancing back to see how she was doing.

She had coped on her own and she had learned to deal with the problems life threw at her without recourse to anyone and without asking anyone's help. She had learned to be contained to the point where sharing herself felt like a mountain that was too steep to climb.

Certainly, sharing anything about her private life with her boss, her *thoughts and feelings*, had never, ever been an option. Now, it felt as though something had shifted underneath her feet, and she would have to claw back lost ground—get them both back to where they had been.

'Shall I cancel the flights and bookings for Naomi?' Her fingers itched for the safety of her tablet which she had been ordered to abandon. 'Will you still be going to Barbados as planned or would you like me to rearrange that trip and reschedule it for later in the month, when you return from Hawaii?'

'Slow down!' He began heading back towards the working part of his office and, in his wake, Ellie heard the laughter in his voice. She gritted her teeth with frustration. He glanced over his shoulder and, sure enough, his lips were twitching.

'Before I do anything, I'll have to run the

gauntlet and face the sea of nosey parkers waiting out here. Wouldn't want to have to bring out the smelling salts because someone's fainted with curiosity. You know as well as I do that some of those computer guys out there can be drama queens…' He paused, one hand on the door. 'And don't despair, Ellie. Give me half an hour, and we'll be back to our usual routine. Boss, secretary…and no lines to be crossed…'

CHAPTER TWO

IT WAS RAINING the following morning when Ellie left her flat for work, a fine, demoralising drizzle that seeped under her lightweight mac and clothes, and settled with clammy persistence on her skin.

She'd had a restless night. The 'back to the usual routine', which James had jauntily flung at her before departing to satisfy the demands of his unashamedly curious staff, had failed to materialise.

At least for her.

The door he'd opened had remained stubbornly open even though she had thrown herself into work for what had remained of the day, barely lifting her eyes from her computer as she'd blitzed all the emails waiting to be dealt with and given ferocious attention to whatever slim backlog of reports there were to go through.

Head bowed, she had still managed to feel the full wattage of his attention on her, however.

He'd perched on her desk, rattling off instructions at his usual breakneck speed, and she'd felt his eyes boring into her, felt his curiosity about those titbits he had managed to eke out of her, opinions she had somehow found herself forced into confiding. She had slid her eyes sideways and been confronted with his black jeans pulled taut over a muscular thigh and had hurriedly had to look away.

So now, hurrying against the blowing, fading summer drizzle, the last thing she expected was to hear a woman's voice calling her name from behind. In fact, she ignored the summons for a few seconds, and only stopped when she felt a hand on her shoulder, at which point she swung round sharply, blinking as the wind blew back the hood of her mac and the rain fell lightly against her face.

She peered up, subliminally taking in the high black shoes, the stupidly long, slender legs, the short red burst of skirt and the black top, all partially concealed beneath the distinctive cream and black check of a designer trench coat. The leggy blonde was enviably dry because she'd had the basic common sense to carry an umbrella with her. So, while Ellie pushed her wet hair from her face and grappled with the hood of her mac, which insisted on doing its own thing, the other woman managed to look only slightly and attractively tousled.

'You probably don't remember me.'

Ellie remembered very well. Not many people could forget Naomi. They had met in passing a month ago, purely by chance, when Ellie had been hurrying to cross the road to get to her bus on the other side. Naomi had been in the passenger seat of James's Ferrari and he had screeched to a halt at the kerb to offer Ellie a lift to wherever she was going. Perfunctory introductions had been made, and in five seconds Ellie had been able to commit to memory the bored blue eyes of his companion, the shiny, long, straight blonde hair swept over one shoulder, the pale golden tanned skin flawlessly smooth and the tiny diamond stud in her perfectly straight nose.

No mistaking the blonde standing in front of her now, although the eyes were more desperate than bored.

'Can you please give this to James? He's not picking up any of my calls and he's not answering my text messages… I know I acted out yesterday, but I love him, and I just want to talk to him…'

'Naomi?'

'I've been waiting for ages in the coffee shop over there to catch you.' Her voice wobbled and she breathed in deeply. 'I know he'll go spare if I show up at his office, and it's just not me to lurk by his house waiting for him to get home. Plus, I'd never know when to expect him. I just *need* to talk to him…'

Ellie looked at the outstretched hand clutching an envelope and sighed.

'I'd rather not get involved…'

'Please! Look, it's pouring out here, and we're both getting soaked. You just have to *give him the envelope*. That's *all*.' Desperation had morphed into the natural state of command, which was often the default position of the very beautiful, and Ellie reluctantly took the envelope. In point of fact, *she* was the only one getting soaked and, frankly, she didn't want to stand out in the rain trying to make a point for the next five minutes, getting nowhere.

'Super.' Naomi beamed and stepped back. 'Thanks.'

'I've got to go,' Ellie returned politely. Then she spun round on her heels and bolted for the office with mounting, simmering resentment.

So much for putting behind her the unfortunate business of boundary lines being crossed! So much for returning to the safety of their boss-secretary relationship and relegating that brief lapse of the day before to the past, never again to be revisited!

The slim envelope in her hand was now forcing her to prolong a situation she didn't want, and resentment had turned to fuming anger by the time she entered the converted warehouse that served as James's cutting-edge office.

If she'd had time, she would have been tempted to go straight to the huge courtyard behind the red-brick building so that she could get her thoughts in order. There, with its rose garden and fountain and benches and abundance of trees and plants and shrubs, all cleverly laid out to provide a peaceful outdoor space for his staff in the middle of buzzy East London, she would have had the opportunity to calm down.

However, at a little after eight-thirty there was no time for calming down, and for the first time since she had joined the company she walked straight into James's office without bothering to knock and without bothering with her usual routine of getting rid of her bag and her mac and readying her computer for the day ahead.

'This is for you.' She slapped the envelope on his desk and then stood back with her arms folded.

In the middle of a phone call, James looked up, and Ellie could see for a few fleeting seconds that he just couldn't believe his eyes.

Where was his well-behaved, dutiful PA? The one who was 'mysterious' yet blatantly dull? She felt a kick of satisfaction as she glared at him narrowly, waiting as he took the envelope and gazed at it, eyebrows raised.

'Going to explain what's going on? Or do you want me to play a guessing game?' he asked, ending his call.

He pushed himself away from his desk and relaxed back to look at her. He'd dumped the envelope on the desk without opening it. Ellie had to take deep breaths, because all she wanted to do just at that moment was wipe the lazy, questioning look from his face.

Like the members of staff, he had no time for the formality of suits, but he had a series of meetings later, and for once was dressed the part. His shirt was crisp and white, although casually rolled to the elbows, and his tailored trousers were charcoal-grey and matched the linen jacket which had been chucked on the walnut unit standing against the brick wall.

He looked incredibly sophisticated, incredibly expensive and breathtakingly sexy, but for once her heart didn't skip a beat.

'Guess who I bumped into outside?'

'Ah. So we're going to be going down the guessing game route… How many guesses am I allowed?'

'Naomi.'

He lowered his eyes for a fraction of a second and stilled. 'Ah… And I'm taking it…' he murmured, reaching for the envelope and twirling it absently between his fingers, 'That this is a missive from her?'

'She said she'd been waiting in the coffee shop opposite to catch me because she didn't want to hand-deliver it to you herself. Look, I come here to work. I don't come here to get involved in any tiffs you have with your girlfriends.'

'Sit down.'

Ellie hesitated. She had more to say on the subject, but he was still her boss, and how much could she complain before he began drawing lines? He was notoriously liberal and open-minded with the people who worked with him. He preferred to get results through nurture rather than wielding a whip. A happy employee, he had told her once, was a productive employee, so he made sure his employees were happy.

But she had seen him with difficult clients and wayward suppliers. She had seen the cold face of a guy who sat at the top of the pile. There was very much a steel hand within the velvet glove, and there was no way she intended to antagonise him by giving him an earful about what she thought of being dragged into his private dramas.

If he didn't want dramatics, she could have told him, then he should try and have a straightforward love life. She clamped down hard on the thoughts running wild in her head and did as told.

'I apologise.' He looked at her and for once that easy, watchful charm was missing. 'You're right. You come here to work and everything else is irrelevant. You don't have to tell me that, Ellie. I've had three years to get the message loud and clear. Yesterday, you found yourself forced to share some of your opinions with me, and I expect you're desperate to get the balance back to normal. Am I right?'

Ellie blushed and tore her eyes away from his remarkable face. 'I don't want to be a go-between between you and your girlfriend,' she prevaricated.

'*Ex*-girlfriend. Even if she doesn't want to believe that at the moment, and even though I'm being bombarded with text messages begging for a second chance. You don't need to know any of this because you're absolutely right—being a go-between definitely isn't part of your job description. Believe it or not, the last thing I want is for you or anyone else to get accidentally involved in my private life.'

The blue eyes resting on her were thoughtful and serious. 'The world sees beautiful women on my arm…' He shrugged and smiled wryly. 'The world doesn't get to see what happens between those beautiful women and me. Which is why Naomi's behaviour here yesterday left a sour taste in my mouth. Which is why I am below zero interested to read whatever is in that envelope.'

Ellie hesitated, lured in by the pensive seriousness in his voice, and the feeling that something was being *shared* between them. Which, of course, was an illusion and yet… What he had just said so perfectly dovetailed with what she thought, that she wanted him to expand on it.

'If you don't read it and respond,' she ventured, 'then you might find that she keeps trying to get in touch until you do.'

'And naturally you don't want to be accosted for a second time by a persistent ex.'

'It's not about that. It's just that…problems don't go away because you want them to.' She flushed. 'At least, that's what I think.' If only they did. If only the problems with her mother had conveniently vanished when she'd been a teenager, leaving her to enjoy her youth without the complications of dealing with situations for which she had been ill-equipped. She felt a shocking urge to cry, and blinked rapidly and with some embarrassment, hoping that he wouldn't notice her crazy reaction.

'Perhaps,' she picked up crisply, 'You'd like me to return when you've dealt with…whatever you need to deal with in reply to…er…whatever is in that envelope?'

'Stay where you are. There's something I need to discuss with you.' He slit open the envelope, scanned the contents and then stuck it to one side. 'I can deal with this later. Now. Tell me what your plans are for the next week or so…'

'My plans?' Ellie looked at him, bewildered.

'I was due to head to Barbados to initiate talks with that start-up company in the expectation of closing the deal a bit further down the line, post a certain wedding ceremony in Hawaii…'

'Yes.' Ellie had no idea where this was leading but she would find out in due course. At least they were no longer skating on the thin ice of personal conversation, although she was still toying with what the contents of that envelope might be.

She had seen the other woman's face, had seen the stark desperation there. It didn't take a genius to figure out that whatever had prompted her outburst of the day before had now given way to horror that she might have blown her relationship with London's most eligible bachelor. That said, bombardment by text message was definitely not the way to go to get a point across. Not to someone like James Stowe.

Poor Naomi. Did she think that James Stowe was the kind of guy to do U-turns? Ellie could have warned her not to hold out hopes for any such thing, but *of course* she would never have done that, because none of this was her business.

Cool reason and the sheer habit of keeping herself to herself fought in vain against stupidly inappropriate curiosity. Was there any side to him that was vulnerable? Could any woman get behind that easy charm to find someone deeper?

She tilted her head to one side and did her best to look engaged with what he was saying, but questions were running around in her head, as though released from a Pandora's box. He was saying something about the start-up company in Barbados and she wondered whether she should be flicking open her tablet at this point to take notes.

'Sorry,' she finally interrupted him. 'Could you please repeat what you just said?'

'Have you been listening to a word I've been saying, Ellie? Or did you temporarily lose touch with Ground Control?'

'Of course I've been listening!'

'Then which bit would you like me to repeat?' He raked his fingers through his hair and flicked her an impatient glance that was tinged with just a shade of disbelief, because not paying attention was something he could never usually accuse her of.

'Forget it. I'll start from the beginning. My

plan was to go to Barbados, stay a few days—just long enough to begin the takeover process with the guys over there from Sailstart—and then head over to Hawaii for the wedding at the end of the month. Naomi was going to be in tow, enjoying the hotel she chose, but getting any serious work done with a girlfriend there would have been impossible. So, my plan was to return later in the month for the serious stuff to begin. Following me so far?'

'Please don't be condescending,' Ellie said politely, and he grinned.

'I am very much liking this new version of Eleanor Thompson,' he murmured. 'Can we have a bit more of her?'

His eyes roved over her in leisurely appraisal and Ellie reddened.

Where was the sensible girl with the sensible clothes and the sensible shoes? Why the heck had she been replaced by this outspoken lookalike with rebellious thoughts, a sharp tongue and a devil-may-care attitude that could only land her in trouble?

'But,' he continued briskly, 'getting to the point, I've had a long chat with the boys over there. Did a bit of groundwork on Zoom and everything has been pushed forward. I aim to complete this deal when I'm there, and as you know that will be a critical period, so looks like my trip over there is going to go ahead after all. It'll probably be longer than the original handful of days. The whole circus of lawyers and accountants are going to have to get involved, so it's going to be a couple of weeks rather than a couple of days.'

He frowned. 'No, not a couple of weeks. Scratch that. I need a bit of time to get prepared for Max's big day. Ten days max out there. I'll kill the island-hopping tourist jaunt, so extending the trip shouldn't be a problem.'

'Great.' Ellie plastered a smile on her face. 'I'll make all the arrangements. Shall I keep the booking at the hotel in Barbados? Or would you like me to change it for somewhere else, now that Naomi won't be going with you?' She paused and wondered whether she had got ahead of herself with that assumption. Did she know the faintest thing about men and U-turns when it came to sex? Lust? She'd read enough articles to know that men were capable of doing extraordinarily idiotic things when they started thinking with the wrong part of their bodies.

Discomfort overwhelmed her as her mind hived off at a tangent and, just for a moment, she had a very graphic image of her boss naked, muscular and aroused.

She felt faint. Her body tingled and she was horrified at the dampness that slowly seeped between her thighs. Her breasts were suddenly hyper-sensitive, wanting to be touched.

'Unless,' she croaked, 'you've changed your mind, in which case…er… At any rate, maybe you could let me know. I wouldn't want to presume anything…'

'You're glowing like a beacon,' he pointed out unhelpfully, and Ellie wanted the ground to open up and swallow her whole. She would be very happy to be disgorged at some later point, after she'd got her act together.

'Am I?'

'Naomi won't be coming along,' he said. 'Although, from what I've glimpsed in that letter of hers, she would like nothing more than just that. I'll keep the room and the hotel, but you'll have to book a separate room as well.'

'A separate room?'

'And an additional flight.'

'Of course. I'll need the details of your companion.' Ellie's imagination leapt into instant overdrive. Another leggy blonde? she wondered. How fast could one man move? At supersonic speed, it would seem. Had Naomi's replacement been waiting in the wings all along? Surely not?

'And,' he countered thoughtfully, 'I really should find out whether your passport's up to date.'

'*My* passport?'

'You'll be coming with me.'

'To Barbados?'

'You'll have to make sure that everything's in place for Trish or Caroline to take over the handling of some of your work, although you should be able to keep on top of most of it remotely, and Higgins will fill in in my absence.'

'Why would I be coming to Barbados with you? I'm afraid that's not going to be possible.'

James frowned. '*Not possible* are two words that have no place in my organisation,' he said coolly. 'I run this ship on the assumption that everything is possible. And the reason you'll be coming with me is simple. I'll need my secretary there because, like I said, I've managed to pull things ahead. And no one else is going to do because you know how I work. Originally, like I *also* said, I hadn't planned on finalising anything on this trip. A few preliminary talks and the rest to be clinched at a later date—probably inviting them here for the sake of convenience. But, as things stand, that option isn't on the cards, so yes, you'll be coming out with me.'

'But…' Ellie breathed in deeply and thought two things at once. The first was that she couldn't imagine being with her boss in a tropical setting, even if work was on the agenda. No. Not at all. And the second thing to cross her mind was her mother, whom she planned to visit at the weekend because the depression seemed to be kicking in once again. After those heart scares, Ellie was determined to do everything in her power to keep her mother on an even keel, and that was to be the weekend's mission. Nice walks, pep talks, home-cooked food.

She took a deep breath and ploughed on. 'I do understand that you might want someone there to keep minutes and do all the usual stuff, but I'm really sorry. I can't take that much time out to go away.'

'Why not?' He leaned forward. 'Boyfriend situation? Sorry, but he'll have to take a back seat for a few days.'

'Won't Caroline do?'

'There's no debate around this, Ellie. Unless you have a water-tight reason for not coming, then I'll expect you to do what you're paid to do.'

And there it was, she thought, the unyielding steel that had got him where he was now. When it came to the crunch, he was hard line, and woe betide if she decided to fight him on this. Aside from which, who in her right mind would fight to avoid an all-expenses luxury trip to sunny climes, when there would be no down side at all, because she would be doing the job she enjoyed doing?

She would have to see her mum, though, and

she gritted her teeth and did her utmost to not flinch at standing her ground.

'Of course. But I will need to…have a couple of days off before I go. I'm assuming the time-lines will be the same as they were? I mean, leaving on the same day?'

'Why do you need a couple of days off?' He tilted his head to one side and looked at her with a frown. She could see the cogs in his brain whirring, piecing her together, filling out the bits he had started filling out when she'd opened up to him yesterday.

It was annoying, but she was resigned to the fact that it was inevitable, and he would soon get bored with the game. He had a lively mind, so it wasn't surprising that he was happy to push at a door that had opened a bit.

And did it matter? She'd assumed that their working relationship would suffer if those lines between them weren't drawn in cement, but re-ally, would it?

They would rub along—and, yes, he might know a bit more about her—but there was noth-ing to fear in that.

She shoved aside those uneasy responses she felt when he was around…when he got too close to her…when those sharp blue eyes rested on her for a second longer than they should…

They were where they were. She would just

have to deal with it. She hadn't committed a crime in being a little less of a closed book.

'Shopping, I take it?'

Lost in her thoughts, Ellie looked at him in puzzlement for a few seconds.

'Clothes,' he elaborated. 'You'll need one or two reasonably dressy things to wear in hot weather. I'll be wining and dining my soon-to-be clients in style, so you'll have to dress the part. Shop to your heart's content and put it on expenses.'

'I wasn't going to take a couple of days off to go *shopping*,' Ellie retorted vigorously, without giving it much thought, and he burst out laughing.

'No need to sound so affronted. It was a simple assumption.'

'I...'

'I'm sure Romeo won't mind letting you go for a few days. In this day and age, please don't tell me that you have to take time off so that you can stock up the freezer for him.'

Ellie stared at him with such an appalled expression that he burst out laughing again.

'I would *never* be one of those women who felt they had to *stock up the freezer* for some guy because he was too helpless to look after himself for a few days!'

'Didn't think so. All men should know how to look after themselves.'

'And do *you* do much cooking when it comes to looking after yourself?' she heard herself ask, sweetly sarcastic.

'Don't have to,' he responded without batting an eye. 'I have a top chef on speed dial. Whatever he rustles up will always be so much better than any of my attempts. Why do you need time off, in that case? We really won't be away for very long. If you're worried about your place, I can always get someone to swing by every day and make sure no pipes have burst and the milk bottles aren't collecting outside…'

Ellie sighed. 'It's not that.' Was he going to let it go? Not a chance. Letting things go wasn't in his nature. 'It's just that I was planning on going to see my mother at the weekend.'

She saw the confusion on his face and understood where it was coming from. She was a woman in her twenties, surely the business of a family visit wouldn't be sufficient for her to dig in her heels at taking a few days to work abroad? A visit to a mother wasn't in the same league as a visit to hospital to see someone on their last legs, was it?

'She lives in Dorset. I… She's on her own, you see, ever since my father… Ever since Dad died.'

'I'm sorry to hear that, Ellie. You should have

said something.' He frowned. 'I don't recall you taking time off for a funeral.'

'My dad died before I joined the company. It's a long story but what it comes down to is that my mother didn't deal with the death very well. In fact, she went to pieces. I've had to…well… I've had to look after her to some extent because she's…had a few problems.'

'What sort of problems?'

'This is very boring for you.' She shot him a self-deprecating smile and he shook his head.

'I don't want to ever hear you say anything like that again. Talk to me. What sort of problems?'

This is what he did, Ellie thought. It was all part of his huge personal magnetism. His charm wasn't just superficial, it was bone-deep, because it was rooted in genuine interest. When he asked a question and looked you in the eye, he sincerely wanted to hear the answer.

'She couldn't cope.' Ellie tried to inject some crispness into her voice but there was a telltale wobble there that she couldn't control. 'She started drinking and the drinking got a little out of hand. It took some time for that to be ironed out, and I'm happy that she's no longer dependent on alcohol, but she's very much prone to depression. She felt like my dad's death took away her reason to live. Since he died, she's had a couple of minor strokes, enough for me to worry about what might happen if another occurred. Right now, she seems to be down again. I could hear it in her voice when I spoke to her at the weekend.

'So there. That's the story. I'd planned on visiting so that I could check the situation for myself—cheer her up, maybe arrange for her to come to London.' She laughed, but it sounded more like a croak, and she ended up clearing her throat.

'Don't you have any other family members who could help you, Ellie?'

'I'm an only child. My parents were only children. There's just me.' She looked down quickly so that he couldn't detect the glimmer of tears in her eyes.

'You must have been…just a kid when your father died.'

'I was sixteen. Old enough to look after Mum.'

'Like I said. Just a kid.'

James looked at her, at the defensive set of her mouth. She was trying so hard to be brave and he imagined she'd spent all those years trying hard to be brave. He knew what it felt like to lose a parent when you were still a teenager. He'd lost both of his. Sometimes in the dead of night thoughts of what that had felt like would surface like eels crawling out of hiding places… dark thoughts about the loss and confusion he had felt all those many years ago.

The truth was that, while Max had taken on the role of caretaker, and while his sister had been swamped with attention from everyone, he had floundered. There had been no one there for him. Not really. No one who could understand the void left. So he had filled the void with friends, activity and a dazzling social life. He had used the tactics of distraction to build a wall around his loss and to seal himself off from dealing with the hurt and sense of helplessness.

James rarely dwelled on a past he couldn't change, but thoughts came at him from nowhere. He remembered that feeling of exclusion, of standing on the outside looking in. He'd been about to go to university, and of course he had, but he had been vulnerable—neither wrapped up in protective cotton wool, as his younger sister Izzy had been, nor fuelled with the necessity to hold things together, which had been his older brother Max's role.

From out of the blue, like a clap of thunder on a cloudless day, he remembered how he had fallen for a ridiculously glamorous older woman who had worked at an art gallery in the centre of Cambridge. She had been bowled over by his accent, by the designer clothes and the fast car—

possessions he had always taken for granted. He had been the youthful idiot mistakenly seeking to fill that aching, empty space with the love of a good woman. When he'd told her that he had no idea if he would be able to afford his next meal now that his parents were gone, she'd begun backing away.

He'd been joking, even though he really hadn't known the state of the family finances, only that Max had intimated they weren't as healthy as they should have been. She'd taken him seriously, and even now he wasn't sure just how shocked he'd really been when he'd caught her in bed with his much richer friend. Short, bespectacled, plump Rupert had been over the moon with his conquest.

James had learnt lessons then that had stayed with him for ever. He was very happy to shower money on the women he dated but his heart was something he had no intention of ever giving away. He had rashly given it away once and he wasn't going to make that mistake again. Never again would he allow himself to get emotionally wrapped up with any woman to the extent that he could end up being hurt. No way. *Build your walls*, he had concluded, *and make sure they're impregnable.*

Impatient with his trip down an unpleasant memory lane, he shook his head and focused.

'A lot of responsibility for you at that age,' he mused quietly. 'Especially if you had no one to share the burden with you.'

'I coped.'

'Coping isn't exactly a great way to wile away your teenage years.'

'Some of us don't get given a choice.'

'No truer word has ever been spoken. Yes, of course you can have a couple of days to visit your mother.' He paused and their eyes met. 'If there's anything I can do, I want you to promise me that you'll let me know.'

'Sure.' She stood up and looked at him. 'I'll start sorting out the details now, if you don't mind, and I'll make sure that there's good cover for me when I'm out of the country.'

'Of course you will.'

Letting his guard slip was all well and good in an office in Shoreditch, but no way was it going to happen on a tropical island in the Caribbean…

CHAPTER THREE

ELLIE WAS HIGHLY efficient when it came to James's travel arrangements. She'd had plenty of practice, given his frenetic, country-hopping schedule, and she could book a five-star hotel, in just the right place for whatever meetings he had lined up, with her eyes closed. She knew the kind of thing he wanted wherever he happened to stay. A luxury penthouse, because he liked a lot of space, and nothing near the ground floor because he enjoyed the peace of looking down on a city at night. And wherever in the world he happened to be, he had to have instant access to the double espressos he lived on when he was working flat out.

She didn't know *how* she knew that. She just did. Which meant he must have told her at some point, or perhaps it was just information that had filtered through by osmosis after so long working together.

Barbados was an anomaly, being a business

trip as well as a mini-holiday, so the requirements had been rather different. Her job had been made easier because Naomi had chosen the hotel, simply leaving Ellie with the task of securing just the right suite of rooms for them in the eye-wateringly expensive boutique five-star.

Her passport hadn't left the top drawer in years, so looking at images of sand and sea had been a vicarious taste of a paradise she'd thought she'd never get to see with her own eyes.

But now there was no Naomi on the scene. Instead, *she* would be the one staying at the fancy hotel in the tropical paradise, and it felt unnatural to be booking a room for herself in a hotel his ex-girlfriend had picked out. Her needs were infinitesimally less complex than his but that made no difference because the price of even the cheapest room was astronomical. When the booking had been confirmed, she'd actually closed her eyes, breathed in deeply and felt giddy at the thought of staying at a luxury hotel in Barbados.

She'd thought that a couple of days with her mother would bring her back down to earth with a healthy reality check. In fact, she'd expected Angie Thompson to be aghast at the thought of her going away when she was grappling with depression and might have wanted her to be around. But, to Ellie's astonishment, her mother had perked up at the news that her daughter would be heading off to paradise.

'It'll do you good to get some time away,' she'd sighed, before wistfully recalling happy days when she and Robert had had fun saving their pennies and travelling as much as they could. 'You've done nothing but look after me for years. You're a good girl, Ellie, but you need to spread your wings and enjoy yourself, and a little break would do you a power of good. Believe me, I know how much you've sacrificed for me and I'm really happy you're going to have some time out. Don't worry about me. I'll be fine.'

Bewildered, Ellie had wondered whether her mother had been listening to a word she'd said and, if she had, whether something had been lost in translation.

'It's going to be about *work*, Mum,' she'd said firmly.

'But in such a glorious place. Your dad and I always wanted to go to that part of the world. He'll be smiling down right now to see you getting there…'

'Getting there *to work*. You have *no idea* what a hard taskmaster James is. My nose will be pressed to the grindstone every minute I'm there.'

Could it be that her mother no longer needed

her quite like she used to? For a moment Ellie had felt a little disoriented…had wondered whether looking after her mum had become part of her comfort zone. And were that to be ripped away…well, how would she deal with it? She would have to engage emotionally with the outside world for the first time since her father's death. It had felt scary, and a thought best put on ice for the moment.

'How are you going to be able to work when the sun's shining outside and there's a beach a stone's throw away?'

It was a very good question, but Ellie knew better than to give it too much mental air-time. Instead, with all the arrangements in place, she had ducked any uncomfortable speculation and convinced herself that there was no reason why anything should be different simply because of a change of scenery. She'd worked for James every summer for the last three years, hadn't she, when the sun had been shining down? Since when had a little hot weather got in the way of doing a job?

She wasn't going to be marooned with him on a desert island, was she? The hotel would be full of tourists milling about, and when they weren't working she would be able to happily lose herself in that throng, or escape to her room, where she would be able to catch up on her reading. She had a backlog of books to get through. There was also a state-of-the-art gym at the hotel, and she intended to make full use of the lavish facilities.

She suspected that, with work out of the way, she would be left to her own devices while her charming and determined boss wined and dined the young businessmen he intended to add to his stable. Pursuit, when it came to getting what he wanted, was an art form to him. He had perfected it, and he would happily leave her behind once the nitty-gritty had been dealt with. She was his PA, after all, not Naomi, whom he had probably banked on helping him with the client entertaining. Tall, blonde and stunning would have been a definite asset.

Still, her stomach was clenched with nerves as she paused outside the airport terminal for a few seconds to gather herself. She'd seen precious little of James over the past few days, having returned from visiting her mother. On the one hand, that was good, because it put distance between her and the uneasy inroads he had made into her private life, leaving her unsettled and desperate to re-establish the status quo. On the other hand, it was less good, because now her nerves were racing through her like quicksilver as she briskly made her way to the first-class desk where they had arranged to meet.

For all her inner pep talks, Ellie knew that her

forbidden attraction was a dangerous weakness. She needed the physical strictures of their working office environment to protect her from…herself and her foolish imagination. It was one thing to begin nurturing thoughts of cutting the apron strings that attached her to her maybe no longer quite so dependent parent, but another to engage emotionally with a guy and finding her feet in a world that had passed her by. It was quite another again to nurture any thoughts about a guy who was utterly inappropriate.

Even from a distance, James Stowe effortlessly stood out. So impossibly good-looking but, more than that, so much in control of his audience. Right now, this consisted of several young, attractive women behind the check-in counter and a pilot, all of whom appeared to be absorbed in whatever he was saying. Lounging against the counter, legs lightly crossed at the ankles, hands shoved into the pockets of his pale, linen trousers, James was talking, half smiling, his head inclined, which gave the appearance of rapt attention.

Which didn't mean that he failed to notice her slow approach, because she could see him straighten fractionally, eyes narrowing as he took in her outfit, which, now that she was in the airport and surrounded by the buzz of excited holiday-goers, felt stiffly uncomfortable.

'What are you wearing?' was the first thing he asked as they headed towards the first-class lounge, having checked in.

'My usual,' Ellie countered. This was the first time she'd been to an airport in for ever, and she had never stepped foot into a first-class lounge before.

She did her best to stop her jaw from dropping to the ground at a world fashioned exclusively for the rich and famous. Uniformed staff were there to await their every command. Would they like something light to eat in the restaurant? Perhaps a late breakfast before taking off? Champagne? Cocktails? They were shown to a buffet sideboard where every type of pastry was there for the choosing. Businessmen sat frowning in front of their computers and, here and there, partners and kids lounged around with plates of half-eaten delicacies in front of them.

James barely seemed to notice their surroundings. 'Ellie, we're going to a hot and humid island. You might find your *usual* a little restricting when we get there.'

'I'll be fine.'

'Breakfast?'

'I grabbed a coffee before I left home...' She glanced at him to find him gazing back at her with amusement. 'But maybe a pastry would be nice. What would you like?' How did it work here? she wondered, glancing around. Did she summon a waiter across? Head to the breakfast station herself and hope the espresso machine wasn't as terrifying to operate as it looked from where she was? Or, did she do as she was doing now and stare back at him in a welter of indecision, wondering where her work hat had gone?

'I'd like to find somewhere to sit.' He looked around and then nodded towards the window. 'And,' he continued, leading the way, 'you don't have to fetch and carry for me, Ellie. Yes, you're here in a professional capacity, but I'd like you to relax and not stand to attention because you feel you have to.'

'Of course.'

James frowned but resisted the urge to carry the conversation further.

Why on earth was she wearing a knee-length navy-blue skirt and a white top that was destined to crease within five seconds of take off? And were those *tights*?

Of course, he knew exactly what was going on. The second he had seen her he had known *exactly* what was going on. With one hand guiding a wayward wheelie suitcase, the other struggling with her pull-along, and wearing her neat navy and white work-ready ensemble, she looked very similar to the three women behind the counter who had been flirting with him.

Except she wasn't, was she? She wasn't just smart. She wasn't just his valued secretary who was quick enough to actually follow what he was saying and sometimes even pre-empt him. No, she was much *more* than that, as he had discovered a few days earlier.

And *that* was what she was desperately trying to extinguish by showing up at the airport in her impossibly inappropriate gear. She wanted to remind him that his duty was to forget that little interlude when she had shed her starchy veneer and, possibly for the first time ever, had actually *communicated* with him with heart-felt sincerity.

Surely, she should know that a healthy dose of curiosity had got him where he was now? If he hadn't been curious enough to explore outside of the confines of his family dynasty then he would never have discovered the gold mines that lay in the fascinating world of artificial intelligence and all things of a techy nature. He had taught himself coding as a hobby at university and, by the time he'd emerged with his first class degree in Engineering from Cambridge, he'd been equipped not only to help his brother handle the juggernaut of the company he had brought back from the brink, but to develop his own multi-million-pound empire—

just as Max had branched out to dabble in the world of boutique hotels and the infrastructure that went with it.

He was curious now, and it had briefly occurred to him, when he had watched her walking towards him pulling those cases, her body language advertising in no uncertain terms the fact that she wasn't here of her own choosing, that he had been curious about her for a while.

Curious in a way he had never really been curious about the many beautiful women he had dated over the years. What was *that* about? She'd walked towards him in the terminal and something inside him had recognised a potent attractiveness that was utterly unembellished and desperate to remain hidden. The graceful sway of her body had momentarily thrown him. Was that the first time? he wondered. Or had that awareness always been there, lurking just beneath the surface?

As fast as that thought entered his head, he banished it back to the hinterland. Had that one and only disastrous relationship, into which he had idiotically flung himself in the wake of his parents' death, severed something in him? Had that vital curiosity that propelled relationships been killed after his one youthful misadventure?

Yes, he concluded, and a very good thing too. Like Max, he had learned from a young age that emotional investment was destructive, that it left room for nothing else. He'd had a double dose of pain. Losing his parents and making the wrong choice in a woman a million years ago. The first had been infinitely worse than the second, but both had taught him that to turn away from the unrewarding labyrinth of emotional investment was to be master of your own universe. In his eyes, never losing control was a source of strength that enabled him to rise above the haphazard business of getting wrapped up in emotions.

He decided that he was curious about Ellie because he wasn't involved with her on any level other than the purely professional, and that could only be a good thing. As far as he was concerned, knowing the people who worked for him bred loyalty. He needed loyalty from Ellie because he couldn't envisage such a smooth working relationship with anyone else.

'How is your mother doing?' He nodded in the direction of one of the circulating airport employees and within five minutes coffee had been brought to them, along with an array of pastries. His keen eyes spotted her automatically begin to reach for her iPad and he decided to forestall any work talk, at least until they boarded the plane. He reached for the dainty cup of coffee in front of him and sat back and sipped, looking at her over the rim of his cup.

'I'm assuming that, since you're sitting next to me, there was no cause for concern?'

'She…she seemed fine. Better than I thought I'd find her.'

'What were you expecting to find?' He lowered his eyes, shielding his expression, then once again looked at her, this time thoughtfully. 'I'm not prying, Ellie. I'm conversing. Relax.'

She was as stiff as a board. He watched the slow blush, a delicate tinge of colour staining her cheeks. Yes, he thought, she was startlingly pretty. Where did that sex appeal come from? It was unexpected in someone so demure. Except, he mused, *demure* she certainly wasn't once you scratched the surface.

His eyes drifted lazily over her full, perfectly shaped mouth, over the short, straight nose, the sprinkling of freckles which seemed curiously delicate for someone with dark hair. He shifted, suddenly edgy, and glanced away. But he couldn't stop himself from picking up where he had left off with his visual exploration. Her hair was neat and shiny and straight, and he would bet his house that it smelled of flowers. Aside from what looked like some lip gloss, war paint was notably absent. There was a cool intelligence in her eyes that he thought could be damned sexy…

He thought about what she had told him about herself, those little snippets of information, and his curiosity ratcheted up a few notches.

Quite frankly, it was invigorating.

What was wrong in having a little enjoyment? It was called passing the time of day. It wasn't going anywhere. There wouldn't be the usual chase followed by the inevitable boredom.

Within that framework, he felt a surge of intense freedom. He should have been sitting here with Naomi. In fact, he was relieved that he wasn't. He was especially relieved to be leaving the country, because she had continued to text him despite his lack of response, and he had an uncomfortable feeling that she might just try and confront him in an effort to 'patch this silly nonsense up', as she had intimated in one of her messages. The last thing he needed was to be accosted from behind by an ex who wasn't interested in reading the signposts.

'Were you worried that your mother might not want to carry on living?'

'No!' Ellie was shocked at the suggestion, although it mirrored the fear she had felt all those years ago when her mother had sought refuge in the bottle. She'd never verbalised it and no one else had either. It had been a forbidding, frightening thought that had eaten away at her until she had come to realise that her mother would not go down that road.

'I'm sorry,' he said, softly. 'I didn't mean to upset you. When my parents were killed,' he found himself telling her, 'there was some lightweight counselling on offer, largely targeted at my sister, who was much younger. They insisted on a few sessions with me and that was the question they laboured the most.'

'I can't imagine you lying on a couch talking to a counsellor.' Ellie smiled.

'There was no couch in evidence. I think movies have helped create that myth…' He liked the way she smiled—a shy, catch me if you can type of smile. He'd planned on using his time in the first-class lounge to work. It was what he always did. But this beat work hands down. Her fingers stopped instinctively straying to the sanctuary of her tablet, which was in the computer case she had taken out of her pull-along. It sat between them on the little circular table, next to the pastries and their cups, an officious reminder that chit chat shouldn't be happening.

'I went to one session,' he drawled, 'to encourage Izzy to follow suit. But then I headed off to university, where I found far more pleasurable ways of dealing with the situation. Wine, women and song can prove excellent home remedies.'

The platitude rolled easily from his tongue as he continued to appreciate an atmosphere that was strangely…*compelling.*

Brought back down to earth by that provocative statement, Ellie's eyes skittered towards the tablet again, and James wasn't surprised when she reached for it, straightened, tucked her hair behind her ears and cleared her throat in a telling signal that time was being called on all informal conversation.

So be it. For the time being.

He was scarcely aware of the drift of his eyes over the crisp, impractical shirt that was tucked into the crisp, impractical skirt. Both were so determined to conceal what lay underneath, but neither could quite hide the jut of her breasts or the slenderness of her waist.

He shifted again, restless, and suddenly needing to move.

'Work.' He slapped his thighs and stood up, abruptly bringing all straying thoughts back to heel. 'Let's work on the Ronson deal. It's picking up pace and maybe we can close on it before the flight gets called…'

He'd been bang on the money about the clothes…

The cool air-conditioning on the plane had insulated her from the reality of the scorching heat that assailed her eight hours later, when the plane touched down at Grantley Adams Airport.

The first-class passengers were off the plane first, and as soon as the heavy door was opened the heat poured in like treacle. She immediately began to perspire.

'Let me,' James murmured, lifting down her pull-along from the overhead locker. 'How did you find the flight?'

'Very relaxing,' Ellie said truthfully, largely because, after half an hour of work-related conversation, James had devoted himself to his backlog of emails and due diligence reports. And because their seats were so spacious, separated by a partition, which he had conveniently chosen to shut so that he could focus exclusively on what he was doing.

She had had the entire flight to herself and she had relished her moment in this unfamiliar world of the uber-rich and famous. It was a world of unashamed luxury where a click of a finger brought you anything you wanted, from champagne to chocolate bars. Her seat was so vast that she'd been able to read her book with her legs tucked underneath her, and the press of a button had turned it into a comfortable bed.

This was how the half a percent lived and this was how James Stowe had always lived. He'd been born into money and, whilst there might have been a brief hiccup within that gilded existence, he had spent his life protected against the harsh realities that most people faced on a daily basis. Even the leggy supermodels he dated, household names who graced the covers of so many magazines, were cosseted and moneyed, thanks to their profession.

She thought of Naomi, with her casual acceptance that attention from everyone around her was her given right. No wonder she had taken it badly when she and James had broken up!

His background couldn't have been more different from Ellie's, and she thought that that might be why she found him so mesmerising… why something in her was stubbornly drawn to him even though she valiantly fought it. He was a shiny bauble. Who could blame her if she was occasionally dazzled by him?

'Slept much?' he enquired, and Ellie looked at him from under lowered lashes. He looked bright-eyed and bushy-tailed and raring to go.

'Not at all. Gosh, it's hot.' This was a different world. The hot sun beat down over a flawless blue sky. Even the airport staff scurrying around outside seemed to move at a slower pace, taking their time.

'Tights might not have been such a good idea.'

Ellie flushed. Of course he was right, but she had been so keen to return to the safety of being his PA, and re-establishing her hands-off approach, that she just hadn't stopped to think. Yes, she'd known that it was going to be hot, but she hadn't expected this level of stultifying heat.

'I've never been to this part of the world before.'

'I've only been a handful of times. It's worth exploring, so don't think that you've got to bury yourself behind your computer and work twenty-four-seven. A personal driver will be available at all times.'

Ellie interpreted that statement to mean that she would be able to explore on her own, and that went some way to reducing her levels of simmering anxiety.

They moved quickly through customs and were treated like visiting royalty. Once outside the terminal, they were ushered to a long, sleek car which was waiting, doors open, for their arrival.

Thrust into scenery that was nothing like any she'd seen before, Ellie forgot her nerves. She forgot that he was sitting right next to her. She even forgot that her clothes had now stuck to her like cling film. The blast of the tropics was so beautiful that she wanted to drink everything in on the short drive from the airport to the hotel—a scant half an hour, if that. Everything was so different. The foliage, the open fruit and vegetable stalls they passed, manned by one or two people sitting on tin chairs and fanning themselves, the blue, blue skies and the shimmer of heat over everything. She felt hot even inside the cool, air-conditioned car.

It was almost a shame when the car swerved into the hotel courtyard. She'd seen pictures of the place on the website, and in the flesh it was exactly the same but with people milling around in brightly coloured clothes, stepping into waiting taxis, holding hands and having fun.

Her choice of clothing, worn to remind her that this was *not* a holiday, worn to remind him that this was a *business trip*, felt ridiculous now. It felt prickly and constricting, and for a few wild seconds she felt so out of her depth that she had to stifle a gasp.

She could smell the ocean as she stepped through the archway into the candy-pink hotel, with its bank of coconut trees fanning out over neatly manicured grounds at the front.

'What would you like me to do for the rest of the day?' she asked, turning to him and managing not *quite* to focus on him as he led the way towards the marble reception desk.

'Relax. Go sit by the pool. If you're tired, you can order room service or you can join me in the restaurant. Your choice. At any rate, we meet the guys tomorrow morning.'

'Here?' The thought of room service filled her with delight. She was tired, and spending what remained of the day in her room would give her time to adjust to these new surroundings. It would also give her time to scrutinise her wardrobe and reflect on some of her ill-advised sartorial choices.

'Bridgetown.' He checked them in, then turned to her. 'I don't know about you, but I need a shower.'

'It's so hot,' she agreed.

'You won't be able to wear…' he nodded to her outfit and raised his eyebrows '…any of your suits while we're over here.'

'I… I hadn't expected this amount of humidity. Of course, I'll make sure to dress appropriately.'

'Good, because tomorrow we'll be on a Catamaran for the day.'

'A Catamaran?'

'A twin-hulled sailing boat. My idea. We're dealing with three young guys who live on an island. Seemed a good idea to have the first business meeting on a boat. Besides, I wanted to see the spec.'

'The spec?' Ellie hadn't had to think too hard about the actual venue for the meetings they would be having with the young businessmen. She'd assumed the usual. A conference room in the hotel…a restaurant…maybe one of their houses for an informal dinner. And all with the usual array of lawyers on the side, quills at the ready.

She'd bought an outfit earmarked for each of those scenarios, and a couple of more casual items for exploring the island on her own.

'You remember the super-yacht? We now have it moored in Monaco,' James drawled, not looking at her as he pinged the button to call the lift. 'It's insanely luxurious, but a super-yacht is a super-yacht at the end of the day. Where's the hands-on experience? It has its own speedboat on board if Max or I want to do something a little more adventurous, but at the end of the day it's largely a passive experience. I want to see what a Catamaran has to offer as a hands-on situation. A fleet of them might prove a good investment.'

The brushed steel doors of the lift purred open and they stepped inside. Ellie looked at him and burst out laughing, and he grinned, a slow, lazy smile that sent a bolt of raw awareness racing through her body with the ferocity of an electric shock.

'Can I hear the dulcet voice of reason about to make its appearance?' he purred, lounging against the mirrored panel and staring at her while the smile still played on his lips.

'Someone has to be reasonable on your behalf,' she said primly, but there was a responding smile in her voice and her lips were twitching.

'Why?'

'Because…' He could be so utterly charming that it was easy to have your breath taken away. She was barely aware of the door opening as she followed him out of the lift onto an airy wooden corridor with broad windows overlooking unimpeded views of the sea. 'Because it's crazy to come over here to get hold of a start-up and end up distracted by a fleet of Catamarans.'

'Have you ever known any of my deals to fail?'

'No, but…'

They'd reached her suite without her even realising and now he leant against the door and stared down at her.

'Max was the sensible one,' he murmured, and Ellie's eyes widened as the gap she was trying hard to establish between them started to crumble. 'He took on the responsibility for grabbing the reins and making sure the ship was steered into calm waters. I will be grateful for ever that he allowed me the opportunity to live a little, even if I *have* ended up as part of the sprawling Stowe dynasty.'

He fished a key card out of his pocket, unlocked the door and pushed it open while Ellie stared at him and struggled to come up with a suitable reply to what he had just said.

A sharing of confidences? Or just a passing remark about something that he didn't consider particularly newsworthy? How fragile was the working relationship between them if it could drift off course with a few random, non-work-related remarks?

But, of course, *she* was the one who was obsessed with maintaining distance between them. *She* was the one who was stupidly affected by him because her body remained at odds with her head. She was smart enough to know that nothing in her life had prepared her for a guy like James Stowe. She was certainly smart enough to know that there was a vast difference between being compatible on the work front and compatible on any other front.

'I'm guessing that you won't be joining me for dinner later?'

'I don't think that that's part of my job description while I'm here, is it?'

Ellie had meant to sound light-hearted. Instead she was embarrassed and dismayed at the ungracious, unnecessarily sarcastic tone of her voice.

His lips had thinned and his eyes were suddenly cool. 'You're quite right. It's not.'

'I didn't mean to… What I'm trying to say is that…'

'I can read the writing on the wall as good as the next person,' he said, stepping back so that she felt the sudden drop in temperature between them like a physical barrier. 'I won't force you to socialise out of hours, although naturally, if it's by way of entertaining business contacts, then I will expect you to oblige.'

'Yes, I wouldn't dream…'

'Of course, you'll be paid overtime. I wouldn't want you to think that I'm taking advantage of you because this is not the usual working environment.'

Blushing furiously, Ellie stared down at her feet for a few seconds. There was no point launching into yet another stumbling apology. Where was her much-prized professionalism? She hated the feeling of losing control.

She breathed in deeply, and when she looked at him her grey eyes were clear and calm and she was proud that she had managed to salvage the situation with some dignity.

'Of course. And you didn't allow me to finish. I have no problem entertaining business contacts. I simply meant that this is a first for me, being in a place like this, and I would very much enjoy getting to see a bit of the island in my free time. If I didn't phrase that properly, then I apologise.'

'Now you're beginning to sound as though you're reading from a script. I almost prefer the sniping approach. So, you want time to yourself while you're out here? Not a big deal.' He shrugged, which made her feel foolish for overreacting to a simple dinner invitation.

'To explore.'

'Naturally. I didn't imagine you'd want nights out to go clubbing.'

Ellie had no intention being drawn into rash self-defence at that provocative generalisation, but holding her tongue was harder than she thought, and she fought to bite back the sharp retort rising inside her.

'What time are things due to kick off tomorrow?'

'Eleven sharp in the conference room on the first floor. We need to brainstorm before we meet the guys at one. Bring your tablet. There's a lot we need to get through before we meet them. They're young and, if there's sailing involved, we'll need to make sure we start laying some foundations down before their attention is distracted.'

'Of course.' Ellie thought that this was more like it. Brainstorming with her tablet and laying down foundations in a workmanlike fashion.

She was smiling, back to her usual unflappable self, as he spun round on his heels to call over his shoulder, 'And don't forget, Ellie…ditch the formal gear. We're going to be sailing the high seas for a couple of hours. You might find a skirt, a blouse and some closed-up shoes get a little restrictive.'

He grinned, mock-saluted and sauntered off before she had time to answer.

CHAPTER FOUR

ELLIE APPROACHED THE hotel boutique and glanced around her. Why on earth did she feel furtive? She wasn't about to rob the store! She was a hotel guest in search of a couple of items of clothing. Couldn't be more straightforward!

But she *did* feel furtive. She felt as though she was sneaking around because she knew what James would do if he spotted her slipping into one of the hotel shops in search of some more appropriate summer stuff. He would laugh, and then he would tilt that handsome head to one side, and he wouldn't have to say anything, because *I told you so* would be emblazoned on his face.

Truth was, he'd been right. In her haste and determination to erase the unfortunate lapses of the past few days, by approaching this trip as nothing but a working arrangement with just a change of scenery to contend with, she had foolishly packed all the wrong stuff. She had thought *office* and had gone for summer suits. She had thought *meetings* and had opted for her neat canvas pumps. She had banked on minimum leisure time with her boss and had stuffed in a couple of pairs of shorts and tee shirts.

In the cool darkness of her palatial bedroom last night, with a view of dark ocean through her window and the sound of night-time tropical insects when she opened the window to breathe in the warm, salty air, she had mentally faced up to her paltry choices. So here she was, at ten in the morning, hovering outside an overpriced boutique where she would now be forced to part with hard-earned cash to buy at least a couple of things that would work for a sailing trip on board a luxury Catamaran and probably a fancy dinner out somewhere.

She cringed when she thought about the cut-off denim shorts buried in one of the hotel drawers and the culottes of two summers back, both of which were absolutely fine if they weren't going to be paraded in front of a guy who was accustomed to the women in his company looking as though they had just hopped off a catwalk. In fairness, many probably had.

Ellie knew that she shouldn't care less what he thought of the clothes she had brought with her. Did it matter? Really? She hadn't been employed because she knew the difference between a Chanel jacket and a Moschino coat. She was here because she was great at her job and he wanted her around to help organise the deal, which was something she was adept at doing without any input from him.

She was here because she was efficient, professional and understood the way he worked, and if she had to accompany him to one or two dinners then she would be required to fade into the background for the remainder of the time.

So what if she showed up in her usual navy summer skirt and another white blouse? So what if he found her bland skirts, and even blander shirts, a source of amusement?

Still, it mattered, and she was cross with herself for *how much* it mattered. Enough for her to have slunk into the boutique the very second it opened and emerge forty minutes later clutching two smart black and gold bags containing a selection of clothes she could ill afford.

She diligently stuck to her usual dress code when she met him twenty minutes later, but he was too focused on what needed to be done to pay her much attention, short of asking her, half an hour after they'd begun poring over the detail of profit and loss columns, whether she wanted anything to eat. Say the word and they would bring whatever she wanted to the conference room.

'I had a huge breakfast.' She politely declined.

'And you slept okay?'

'Brilliantly,' she responded honestly. 'I thought I'd be up, with the time difference, but once my head hit the pillow I was out like a light. The suite is amazing and the bed is fantastic.'

Uninvited, she imagined *him* lying in a king-sized bed very much like the one she had fallen asleep in, and from that diving point she plunged into her newly awakened imagination which was threatening to get completely out of control. She reined it in with effort, inwardly cursing the way three years' worth of self-control around him had been demolished in the space of a few days and a handful of unedited conversations.

She felt the pinch of her nipples against her sensible cotton bra, an unwelcome dampness between her legs, and suddenly the room, which had been perfectly fine moments before, was uncomfortably hot. Too hot. She wanted to fan herself.

Instead, she hastily poured herself a glass of cold water from the jug that had been brought in for them and drank thirstily.

Her eyes slid down to his khaki shorts, just the right length to draw her eye to his muscular thighs and strong calves. His expensive tan designer boat shoes looked well-worn, as did his faded blue and cream polo shirt, and yet as a package deal he looked a million dollars. Money, she thought, bought freedom. And that included freedom from caring what impression you made on other people. It was that very indifference that made him stand out. He wasn't obliged to do anything he didn't want to do and that was all too apparent in his body language. People bent over backwards to please him all the more because he didn't encourage it.

After the stormy break-up, Naomi had bent over backwards to reinstate herself. Ellie knew that because she had taken three calls in the space of a single day before they had left for Barbados, and had, thankfully, been legitimately able to tell the other woman that James wasn't around.

'Believe me,' she had said truthfully, 'If he was in the office, I would transfer you. Perhaps,' she'd added with a twinge of satisfaction, 'You could try his mobile. I'm sure he'd be very happy to take your call.'

She had no idea whether he had taken any calls from his ex, and if he had whether he'd been happy to take them, but that wasn't her concern.

'I have a few calls to put through before I meet our clients,' he said when they'd finally finished fine-combing through the details. 'Unexpected and essential, I'm afraid. Will you be okay making your way to the Catamaran on your own and entertaining the guys for a few minutes if I'm late?'

Ellie watched as he absently looked at something on his phone before helping himself to water, looking at her over the rim of his glass as he drank.

'Of course.' It would be a chance to take in a bit of her glorious surroundings without his stifling presence next to her, consuming all her attention. She smiled. 'Is there anything I should know about our contacts? Aside from the fact that they're young?'

'Nothing.' He grinned back at her and began heading for the door. 'Young computer whizz-kids...probably more brains and energy than common sense. I'm guessing your experience at my company will serve you in excellent stead when it comes to dealing with these three—and don't worry. I won't leave you in the lurch for too long.'

'I'm not worried.' She preceded him through the door and caught a whiff of his woody cologne.

'That's my girl,' he murmured, glancing down at her. 'I can always depend on you.'

Ellie wondered why that sounded ever so slightly patronising rather than complimentary. Dependability was what she was about, so why would she feel *criticised*? Since when had she become so sensitive to every passing remark? How tenable would her job be if she ended up brooding over everything he said and mulling over every expression that crossed his face? Not to mention her imagination suddenly deciding to take flights of fancy at the drop of a hat.

'Thank you,' she returned, drawing back to look at him. 'Will you text and let me know if you're going to be late, and if so how late?'

'I will most certainly do that,' he murmured.

Ellie ignored the lazy amusement in his drawl. 'And should I try and get anything together before I get there?'

'Anything like what—food? Drink? Dancing girls and circus performers?'

'Very funny.' She clicked her tongue with exasperation and his grin broadened. 'Honestly,' she muttered, 'You're impossible sometimes.'

'You're the only one who can do that.' He was looking at her with a veiled expression that was just the right side of serious, and when their eyes met she had to control a shiver of treacherous awareness.

'Do what?'

'Put me in my place.'

A wave of confusion crashed over Ellie and she fidgeted, skewered by the barely readable expression in his eyes. 'And don't tell me that's something you like!' she joked shakily.

'You'd be surprised.' He raised his eyebrows but that lazy intensity was still in his eyes, still sending shivers down her spine. 'Maybe we all need someone who's not scared to put us in our place. Especially powerful men like me.'

He grinned, breaking the spell, and Ellie felt her body sag with relief.

He hadn't meant that. Her imagination was at it again, amplifying his words. So much of what he said was part and parcel of his enormous, unconscious charm, a heady mix of intense focus wedded to light-hearted teasing that got under your skin and gave you goose bumps.

She thought about what he had told her about the aftermath of his parents' death. About Max taking hold of the reins and Izzy finding the warmth of support which had left *him*... Had he dealt with loss by becoming the guy who seemed just fine under the dazzling personal charm?

'I'll make sure what we've discussed this morning is collated and ready to be emailed.' She changed the subject, keen to get away. 'And I'll make sure I'm at the designated spot on time. No need to rush if you're busy. I'm more than capable of handling the situation until you get there.'

She smiled politely and thought that it might

be quite relaxing to get used to the businessmen without James lurking in the background, unsettling her.

If the deal came to fruition—and it almost certainly would, because everything he touched turned to gold—then *she* would inevitably be the one most in contact with the new partners, because that was usually the way it worked out. James clinched his massive deals, started the wheels churning, oversaw everything until it was safe to retreat, then left her and his various CEOs to fine-tune the details and handle the after-care. Then all those computer geniuses would move into action, taking the bare bones of the programmes handed to them and expanding them into apps that always captured parts of the market no others had captured before.

It would be worthwhile finding out a little about the guys she would end up dealing with because it always made for an easier relationship.

She thought of the prim and proper clothes she had dragged along with her and breathed a sigh of relief that she had had the chance to blow some of her money on a couple of things that would make a better impression in the casual tropical setting. She had not given sufficient thought to it when she had flung open the doors of her wardrobe in London.

For three years, surrounded by her brainy,

wild and whacky colleagues, she had stuck rigidly in the background, had stuck to the persona she had moulded for herself. Years of anxiety, years of looking after her mother, years of sublimating her own grief in the face of bigger concerns, had conferred a serious maturity on young shoulders.

Here, though, under these hot, turquoise skies and velvet, starry nights, she would stop being that careful young woman, risk-averse and taking no chances.

So her boss thought she was Little Miss Efficient and Ever So Slightly Dull?

Well, it would give her a kick to prove to him that there was a bit more to her than knee-length skirts and sensible shoes…

The short taxi ride from the hotel to the marina, where the Catamaran was waiting for him, was an uncomfortable one because the air-conditioning in the car wasn't working. By the time James had weaved his way through the crowds towards the yacht, he was dripping in perspiration and running thirty minutes behind schedule.

Thank God he could rely on Ellie to hold the fort until he arrived.

Thank God that, whatever stirrings of curiosity he had felt about the solid, dependable woman who had worked for him for the past three years, she was, underneath it all, the mainstay of his working day.

Nothing, he thought as he scanned the marina for the luxury Catamaran he had rented for the day, could ever put a dent in that unflappable personality. She was so adept at keeping a cool grip on whatever situations might occur, such as the one in which he currently found himself.

Annoyingly late.

En passant, he noted the bustle around him, the glitter of the sea, the soporific bobbing of all the yachts moored in the marina, and overhead the dazzling blue of the sky.

For a few seconds, he stopped dead in his tracks, living for the moment. It was not something he often did. Life was busy. Running an empire left little time to look around. He was a man accustomed to life being lived in the fast lane but now… 'Fast' was not what this spectacular island was about, and for a few minutes he savoured the pleasure of the dramatic scenery.

Around him and behind him lay the capital, Bridgetown, awash in sun as dense as treacle. Everyone chatted happily, bustling between buildings that ranged from imposing, older buildings to sleek, modern towers, interspersed with brightly coloured shops and offices. The air smelled of the salty ocean, the burning sun and the aromas of food wafting out from doorways of cafés and little restaurants sprinkled along the promenade that ribboned along the sea front. Along the promenade, with its intricate iron railings, handy to lean against and contemplate the endless ocean, several shops spilled out their stash of brightly coloured clothes, hats and bags for sale, appealing to locals and tourists alike.

He tried to picture Naomi in this setting and was intensely relieved that things had crashed and burned. There was no way he would have been able to devote any quality time to this incredibly satisfying deal, making sure the businessmen he was on the way to meet were kept sweet. He imagined she would have wanted his full, undivided time to escort her to beaches and restaurants where she could be on show.

Ellie, on the other hand…

He headed towards the promenade, moving past little groups sitting at wooden tables, dining out in the sunshine.

He was running late, which was a pain in the neck, but he could rely on Ellie doing everything that needed to be done—from pouring glasses of whatever had been provided by the five-star caterers supplied by the hotel, to taming the young men, and adroitly introducing them to what their roles would be once the company became his. For they would retain some shareholding, with his blessing.

Right now, she would be toeing just the right line between chatty and polite and professional and efficient. He wondered which of her 'dressed for a normal working day' suits she would be wearing, and found himself absently toying with the fascinating notion that she might have leapt out of her comfort zone straight into something that wasn't grey or blue.

In contrast to Naomi, he realised, Ellie, with her quietly unostentatious clothes and neat appearance, didn't *jar*.

Up ahead, he spotted the Catamaran, which he had rented for the day, with a hold on it in case he needed it again. It was in a league of its own, gleaming black, its massive twin hulls holding bedrooms, a dining area and somewhere to relax away from the blistering sun.

Maybe, he mused idly, he should take a break from the high-maintenance woman with all her tiresome needs, and demands which always ended up surfacing sooner or later. Maybe he should opt for *soothing*. He worked all the hours God made and his life was high octane, high stress and high risk. Maybe soothing would work for him. Were there any soothing women in his proverbial little black book? None that he could think of.

Disgruntled mood disappearing with every step closer to the Catamaran, James was in high spirits as he boarded the waiting yacht. No one was on deck, which meant that work was probably under way in the cool, below-deck room which he had specified had to multi-function as a conference area.

He heard voices as he nimbly hopped onto one of the hulls, steadying himself on the railing.

Voices and laughter.

He had no idea what he'd been expecting, but whatever it had been certainly wasn't what greeted him when he ducked down into the spacious living area, with its in-built cherry-wood seating and the matching sideboard groaning under the weight of food and drink, courtesy of the very capable catering staff at the hotel.

The businessmen were there but business didn't appear to be under discussion. Bottles of beer nestled in hands and used plates told a tale of lunch already having been taken. Unless the business in question involved the uproarious telling of jokes, this was a social gathering, not the work situation he had envisaged.

And Ellie…

He wasn't sure what shocked him more—the fact that she was wearing a colourful sarong and a vest top that advertised a body that had largely been invisible in all the time she'd worked for him, or the fact that she was drinking a bottle of beer.

What the hell was going on here?

Why was she drinking? Of course he'd seen her drink before. But always wine. A civilised glass of premium Sancerre at one of the company get-togethers. He'd never had her down as a beer girl!

And where was the tidy skirt? The neat blouse, top two buttons daringly undone because of the searing heat? Where were the sensible shoes?

And she was *laughing*!

James was taken aback by the depth of his shock when, taken individually, none of the things were in themselves shocking. People wore small clothes in hot weather. People drank beer. People laughed. What was the big deal?

Furthermore, hadn't he encouraged her to dress for the weather? Hadn't he been guilty of gently teasing her about her prim outfits, his tone of voice encouraging her to dare to break the mould?

Well, she had broken the mould, *and then some*. This was a different Ellie. This Ellie was confident and assured, and her covert sexuality was out in the open big time. This Ellie was a woman he had not glimpsed before. She was positively modest in her dress compared to the women he dated and yet she still had the irresistible appeal of a siren. He had to drag his eyes away from her and kill a jealous suspicion that he was probably not the only one appreciating the assets on view. He didn't do jealousy—never had, never would!

From where she was sitting, relaxed but still fully in charge of the three high-spirited young men who were so much like the guys at the office, Ellie was aware of her boss before he even appeared at the door.

Maybe, Ellie thought, she'd been waiting for him, her attention riveted to that door, her body laced with tension underneath the chat and the laughter.

Yes, this was work, but not as she had ever known it. She had ditched the uniform with a surge of confidence, spurred on by the fact that all her boss's remarks had somehow made her feel dull and unexciting.

She had felt a thrill of pleasure earlier when she had stood in front of the hotel mirror and inspected the reflection staring back at her. Indeed, she had had trouble recognising herself. Had all those years of heavy responsibility really made her forget how young she still was? She had had to grow up fast to deal with the fallout from her father's premature death. Had she somehow gone from teenager to middle-aged woman, skipping all the fun bits in between?

The brightly coloured sarong and the small

turquoise top were hardly risqué, but she'd *felt* risqué in front of that mirror. She'd *felt* what she was—a twenty-something girl with every right to have fun.

Now, as James's eyes swept over her, she refused to be cowed into thinking that she should have dressed as he'd no doubt expected.

Antony, Victor and Sol raised their beer bottles in welcome as Ellie gracefully rose to her feet, bottle in her own hand, and made the introductions.

She moved towards James as he moved towards her, tentatively, to accommodate the faint rocking of the boat as it bobbed on the water.

'Not quite what I was expecting to find,' he murmured truthfully, just low enough for her to hear, but his words spoken in passing because he was already beginning to engage with the young men.

Ellie felt a spurt of unaccustomed anger. Had he expected her to be seated with her notebook and pencil? Slapping down anyone who spoke out of turn? Maybe banishing them to the naughty corner?

Yes, he had! Because she was the efficient PA, never flustered, never out of her depth, always available.

She was swamped with a mixture of simmering rebellion and uncharacteristic recklessness brought on by her slinky clothes and the complimentary looks from the young lads. They were looking at her with the sort of male appreciation of which she had been starved for longer than she cared to remember, and she refused to fade into the background as usual.

She chatted and laughed and helped herself to another bottle of the local lager when it was offered. She knew her stuff and she knew exactly when to focus the minute the conversation turned to work. All the information she had meticulously filed in her head was at her fingertips, and she could deal with facts and figures even after her two beers.

For the first time in ages, Ellie threw herself into having fun. They had hired a skipper for the day, and she felt a burst of freedom as the Catamaran took on the wide blue sea.

A little while later up on deck, with conversation swirling around her, she sat with her knees drawn up and gazed at the limitless horizon. The yacht was moving at a rate of knots and the wind blew her hair around her face. The sky was the purest of dazzling blues and, as the boat left shallow water for deeper ocean, the sea was a dark navy, broken by the white froth of ripples from the wind and the ocean currents.

Victor perched next to her, bare-backed and with no thought whatsoever about sun block, and chatted to her about the turtles you could swim with, and the sting rays you could spot shimmering like pancakes in the sand, if you decided to go snorkelling. He gave her more information about the ins and outs of cricket than her brain could hold, and told her that she had to try Mount Gay rum, which was the best in the world.

At some point, when she had moved on from beer to bottled water, the skipper dropped anchor and everyone except her took the plunge into the bottomless sea.

Antony… Victor… Sol…and James.

Sitting and watching from the deck, hiding behind the sunglasses she had thankfully brought with her, Ellie looked at her boss, so much taller and so much more muscular than the other three. His body was a work of art. Solid packed muscle and a six-pack that was testament to power sessions at the gym. The sun would lighten his hair. It was already deepening his colour.

His trunks, black and halfway down his thighs, were hardly the stuff to fire the imagination, yet she felt weak at the sight of them and the heavy bulge of what was underneath.

The sun was setting by the time the skipper lifted anchor and they began heading back to the marina. Darkness was settling fast. One minute the glare of the sun had mellowed and then the orange orb began to sink on the horizon, turning the skies first indigo, then velvet-black.

High spirits had given way to mellow, serious conversation, and she had taken a lot of notes by the time the yacht drew up to its mooring, working on her iPad and storing up an equal amount to transcribe later.

'I'll take it from here,' James told the skipper. When Ellie made to follow the guys off the yacht, he stretched out one arm, a signal for her to stay put.

'What…what's going on?' she asked as the last of the guys hopped ashore and James, to her consternation, kicked the yacht back into life, nudging it expertly into open water.

Of course he could skipper a yacht, she thought, compulsively looking at his strong, veined forearms as he guided it with one hand. If it came to it, he could probably fly a plane through the eye of a hurricane.

'We need to talk.'

'Perhaps it could wait until tomorrow morning?' She glanced over her shoulder to where the twinkling lights and safety of crowds on the promenade were being left behind.

The pleasant effect of beer was beginning to wear off, and as the yacht picked up speed, heading in the same direction along the west coast as earlier, she felt a shiver of forbidden excitement.

She didn't want this! Hadn't she already made it clear that her time would not be consumed with work-related issues simply because they weren't in an office?

And yet…

There was a sense of simmering danger in the air that made the hairs on the back of her neck stand on end. They were so far away from *normal*. Now, cruising along the shoreline, the panorama was quite different, everything plunged into inky shadows and distant, looming shapes. Yet it was barely any cooler than it had been during the day, with just the faintest of cooling breezes as he slowed the yacht to a soft stop, where it bobbed lazily on the calm water.

When he turned to her, she could only make out his shadowy outline. The angles of his beautiful face were hidden and she couldn't read the expression in his eyes.

'This is a bit dramatic, isn't it?' She laughed a little nervously because it was hard to get a grip on his mood. 'I mean, if you want to talk about what was said about the prospective deal, then we could have…um…caught up in the morning. I may have had a couple of beers, but I remember every word that was said.'

'I would expect nothing less.'

'Then…what's the problem? Why are we out here?'

* * *

James thought that that was an excellent question. Unfortunately, he couldn't quite find as excellent an answer, because the hell he knew why he was out here. He just knew that the past few hours on this Catamaran had been a hellish ordeal mentally, trying to channel her back into the predictable box from which she had unexpectedly sprung. Astonishment at what she'd been wearing, at her drinking and at her easy, sexy confidence with those guys had kick-started all sorts of shocking, taboo urges inside him. He had to get it out of his system, and that was frustrating, because he wasn't sure what exactly it was he had to get out of his system.

'You… I wasn't expecting to find you dressed in a sarong and a tiny top,' he opened, and was immediately appalled at the censorious tone of his voice. Since when had he become a feudal overlord?

'Sorry?'

He raked his fingers through his hair and looked uncomfortably at the slight figure in front of him.

The small top curved over her perfectly small, rounded breasts, the sarong dipping just enough to expose her slim, flat stomach and a glimpse of slender leg every damn time that sarong flared open a little.

Since when had she become the sexiest woman on the planet? Had he registered that before and somehow managed to sublimate it? He had been the victim of a raging libido for the entire time they had spent on the yacht. It had been a mammoth effort not to look at her, and even a long swim in the ocean hadn't been able to douse the sudden fire that had ignited inside him. For once, his formidable will power had not been able to rescue him from feeling like a horny teenager.

'I'm not saying you can't wear whatever you want to wear,' he said in a roughened undertone. 'I'm just saying you caught me by surprise…'

Ellie's mouth fell open. 'You've driven this boat out here so you can tell me *that*?' She glared at him. 'And should I be grateful that you haven't objected to my dress code?'

'Of course…' James tried to rescue the farcical situation with some semblance of rationality. 'It would be an opportune time to consolidate what…has been said…'

'You told me to wear appropriate clothes. I'm wearing appropriate clothes! And, when it comes to work, we could easily discuss that tomorrow! You just *don't approve* of what I've chosen to wear! Which, *incidentally*, is a whole lot less dramatic than what most girls my age would be wearing on a boat in the tropics!'

'Did I say that I didn't approve of what you're wearing?' James retorted with a hint of defensiveness. Where was this coming from? He had no idea, and that lack of control was messing with his head. He couldn't remember a time when he'd actually cared about what clothes any woman chose to wear. Unconvincingly, he tried to tell himself that he was being perfectly reasonable in this instance because she wasn't just any woman, she was *his PA*. She was *paid* to look the part! Her role wasn't to turn him on until he found it impossible to think straight…

'You don't have to,' Ellie said coldly. 'You're accustomed to seeing me one way and one way only.'

'You've hit the nail on the head,' he muttered. He spun round to stare at the dark sky and the even darker sea. He felt hot and uncomfortable in his skin. He felt…*aroused* at the sight of her. He wanted to touch her, and he didn't know what to do with the feeling, so he ground his teeth together and glared at her.

'As of tomorrow, I will return to my normal dress code,' Ellie managed to bite out with such stiff politeness that he knew she was fighting hard not to shout at him. 'And I'll make sure to bring out the *appropriate* stuff when you're not around to disapprove.'

'Don't,' he said brusquely. 'You think I disapprove. Maybe I approve too much.'

His words hung in the air between them, as dangerous as a match being tossed onto dried leaves.

'I don't understand,' Ellie said confusedly.

'Don't you? I couldn't take my eyes off you. Okay, so maybe you're right. Maybe I *have* been accustomed to seeing you in one way and one way only. Maybe I like this break with tradition a little too much for both our good.'

James had never envisaged himself in this position. Had he ever thought about her that way? Maybe. He didn't know. She'd always got under his skin in a strange kind of way. Had it been a simmering attraction he had always refused to acknowledge? At any rate, the words were out and he was unrepentant. In fact, he felt oddly calm.

'I don't know what you're saying,' Ellie whispered.

'Don't you? Then allow me to spell it out. You sat there on this boat, sexy as hell, and I wanted you. It wasn't just the clothes. I saw a different woman and I wanted her. I want her right now. I can't get any clearer than that, can I, Ellie? I want to kiss you. I want to make love to you. Right here, right now, on this boat in the middle of the sea…'

CHAPTER FIVE

ELLIE GASPED HER shock, but through the shock dark excitement coursed with mercurial speed through her veins. She took a couple of steps back, her breathing shallow and rapid, her eyes pinned to the dark shadows of his face.

This wasn't what she'd been expecting. When he'd dispatched everyone and announced that he wanted to take the Catamaran back out to talk to her, she'd put two and two together and come to the vague conclusion that he was keen to discuss what had been agreed during the course of the afternoon on the yacht. That he'd opted to take the boat back out because that was the type of guy he was—he just wanted to have a go sailing it. She suspected that the only reason he'd hired a skipper in the first place was because he hadn't wanted the distraction of being behind the wheel when there was business to get through.

But this…! No! She couldn't possibly! She wasn't built for something like this…she needed *stability* and *boundaries*. Lose those and what next? It would be as perilous as diving head-first into a whirlpool! She needed *control*, yet…

Every bone in her body was melting and she was grateful for the cover of darkness so that he couldn't see the tell-tale trembling of her body. Shameful arousal was a heat pouring through her, and she felt the tingling pool of dampness between her thighs, which made her want to rub them together.

She hugged herself and stared at him.

He was her boss! This shouldn't be happening! Why was it happening? Was he even being serious? She was hardly in the league of all his ex-girlfriends, with their ridiculously long legs and supermodel figures.

A thousand fevered questions raced through her head, but her tongue seemed to be glued to the roof of her mouth and all she could do was stare at him, dumbfounded.

'Tell me about it,' he grated.

'Is this some kind of joke, James?'

'Do I sound as though I'm kidding?'

'But… I work for you! And it's not even as though I'm your *type*!'

'Think I'm not grappling with the same mystery?' He shifted, for once lacking his usual poise. He looked at her, looked away, looked again and then kept looking. 'I'm not a believer in mixing business with pleasure…'

'I know,' Ellie said faintly. Was this conversation really happening? Yes, it was, because there had to be a reason she was finding it hard to breathe. 'You don't like your girlfriends invading your work space, never mind occupying a permanent space in it.'

'All true,' he growled, unconsciously taking a small step towards her, closing the distance. 'and, as an aside, don't think that because I date tall blondes that you're not sexy…'

'We need to stop talking like this,' Ellie whispered shakily. 'We'll head back to shore and pretend this conversation never happened.'

'You think it's going to be that easy?'

'It will be because I'll chuck these clothes to the bottom of my suitcase and return to my boring skirts and tops.'

'And that's why you're sexy.'

'Why? What are you talking about?'

'You say things that make me smile. Do you honestly think that a change of wardrobe is going to quench what I'm feeling? You make me smile and, when you add in a sharp brain, you have a killer combination. I looked at you earlier, poised…confident…at ease with every bit of technical conversation being tossed around… You can't imagine what a turn-on that was.'

He paused and then turned away to grasp the hand rail that ran round the edge of the boat. 'I need to cool off.'

Ellie didn't say anything. Her head was buzzing. She wanted all this nonsense to stop immediately! But she also wanted him to keep on talking, feeding her ego and sending her nervous system into a tailspin.

She *liked* what he was doing to her and that terrified her. The door that had been nudged ajar between them had now been kicked wide open and, whilst she was desperate to get it shut again, whilst she *knew* she had to get it shut again, a wilful part of her couldn't help but toy with the idea of touching him.

She'd wanted to, hadn't she? Hadn't she thought about that in the early hours of the morning, caught in that pleasant place between sleep and wakefulness, when thoughts were allowed to roam free? Yes, *of course* they weren't compatible, not *at all*, but still, acknowledging that did nothing to kill the surge of desire inside her.

'I need to have a swim.'

'You can't!'

But he was already stripping off his tee shirt. After swimming off and on during the day, he had left his swimming trunks on. He was ready to dive into the sea, except this time there was no blue sky above or transparent water lapping the sides of the Catamaran. Now, the sea was threateningly deep, dark and fathomless. Ellie watched in fascinated horror as he moved swiftly to the side of the boat, eschewing the shallow steps on each hull that would have made for a slower adjustment to the coldness of the water.

He dived straight in and disappeared. *Of course he would surface!* She had watched from the sidelines as he had swum earlier on, mesmerised by the graceful fluidity of his lean body slicing through the water, his strokes effortless and powerful at the same time It was so dark that she could barely make out anything. She certainly couldn't make out any surfacing shape and her panic began rising the more she peered into the darkness, hoping to see his silhouette.

The twin-hulled, squat shape of the boat made for a very solid, safe vessel but she now wondered whether he had misjudged the width of it, so much broader than a typical small yacht, and had tried to surface only to find his head bumping against the bottom of the boat. Things could get confusing when you couldn't see clearly and you were in unfamiliar surroundings. What could be more unfamiliar to someone whose stamping ground was the concrete jungle than an ocean, at night, in the middle of the tropics?

Frantically moving from bow to stern and scouring the flat, dark ocean mass, she yelped when she heard his voice behind her. In fact, it took her a couple of seconds to recognise his voice at all, and her heart was in her mouth when she whipped round to see him standing in front of her.

'Where the *heck* have you been?' She was pressed against the railing, gripping it for dear life. The gentlest of night breezes wafted her fine hair around her face and she impatiently pushed her hand through it.

'Swimming.'

He'd fetched a towel from the deck somewhere and was drying himself.

'Yes, I know you've been *swimming*!'

'Then why the rhetorical question? Let's go below deck. I need to get into some dry clothes.'

He spun round on his heels and began heading down to the living and sleeping quarters, ample enough, as she had discovered, for eight people to move around comfortably without getting in one another's way.

'Were you worried?'

The spacious quarters now seemed cramped as he slowly turned to look at her, having flung the towel on the table which nestled in the centre of a fitted L-shaped banquette.

The galley, the saloon and the helm station all flowed into one huge open space in this area. Ellie's legs felt like jelly but, whilst she was desperate to sink onto the padded leather banquette, his dark blue eyes, so dramatic with their lush, dark lashes, skewered her to the spot, making movement impossible.

Down here, the dark, warm night and the inky black ocean were no longer pressing around them. Only the gentle undulating of the boat was a reminder that they were on water.

'I didn't see you surface,' she said thinly. 'Of course I was worried! Anyone would have been in my situation?'

'And what situation is that?'

He'd towel-dried and slung on his dry tee shirt, but the swimming trunks were still on, clinging to his muscular thighs, and she had to steel herself not to look.

One glance and who knew what kind of unwelcome physical responses would be surging through her already heated body?

The electricity between them sizzled and she wasn't going to do anything to ratchet it up further.

He fancied her... He wanted to touch her...to kiss...to make love...

Those words were now lodged in her head and how on earth was she going to get rid of them? There were only so many times she could keep telling herself that they weren't suited. Maybe she had become reliant on her role of carer.

Maybe she had hidden behind that role even when her mother had stopped needing her quite so much… Maybe, *just maybe*, she had become fearful of taking all those risks involved with dating guys and just having fun. But, if things had to change, then surely not with a man who had 'heartbreaker' stamped all over his forehead! Her breathing was staccato, uneven, as she continued to flounder helplessly.

'Drink?'

'No!'

He'd moved to the ingenious wine bottle holder that was built into a concealed walnut drawer.

'You're not going to be able to get the boat back…' She followed his movements with avid, treacherous concentration.

James paused, wine glass in one hand, and shot her a slow, lazy smile that made her toes curl. He'd cooled down and was obviously back in control of the situation. Was he sufficiently in control to realise that anything between them, *anything*, would be a disaster?

'Oh, ye of little faith…' He poured himself a glass of red and strolled towards her to sit on the banquette and pat the space next to him. 'You didn't answer my question,' he prompted softly. 'What situation?'

'Huh?' She ignored the space next to him and

sidled to sit facing him instead. The soft lapping of water against the side of the boat was a barely discernible noise, more felt than heard. In here, the silence was thick with tension.

'You said that anyone *in your situation* would have been worried sick…'

Ellie noted the way he had tacked the word *sick* onto his sentence, turning it into quite a different emotion.

'Do you mean,' he continued thoughtfully, 'that anyone trapped on a boat would be worried if they ended up on it alone because they might be stranded at sea until someone came along and rescued them?'

'Of course not! I'm not a helpless damsel in distress! If I were on this boat alone, I'm sure I would be able to somehow get it back to shore.'

'Maybe, then,' he mused, sipping his wine and looking at her with the same pensive expression that gave no guidance as to exactly what was going through his head, 'you were concerned that, if your boss disappeared off to that great watery graveyard in the sky, your future as a highly paid worker bee might be on the line. I'll admit there are few companies in London that could rival the working conditions at my place, not to mention the pay…'

'That's a crazy thing to say!' She whitened, thoughts zooming to him involved in any kind of accident, feeling sick at the very thought. 'That's not why I was worried! I was worried because… because…'

'Because,' he murmured, looking at her steadily, his dark eyes boring straight into her, addling her, 'You have feelings for me that go beyond the usual, predictable boss-secretary relationship, don't you…'

It wasn't a question, it was an assumption, and she opened her mouth to deny it but nothing emerged.

'You're attracted to me, whether you want to admit it or not. You're as attracted to me as I am to you. Maybe we might not have said anything before, when we were in London, imprisoned in the routine and normality of my office there, but here we are.'

'No,' Ellie whispered weakly.

'Alone…' he continued with the remorseless determination of a battering ram. 'In this Catamaran, out in the tropics, with nothing but the deep, dark ocean beneath us and the deep, dark skies above us…'

'Stop, please.' She barely recognised her voice. Gone was the no-nonsense firmness which represented the backbone of her relationship with him. In its place as a wavering, pleading hesitancy that exposed all her weaknesses.

He'd said that she had feelings for him.

He'd summed that up as meaning that she was physically attracted to him.

That wasn't the whole story, though, was it? And therein lied the danger. But, sitting here, the danger was sidelined by the tremendous drag on her senses evoked by what he was saying and the way he was looking at her.

'Come sit next to me.'

Ellie hesitated and he smiled, smelling victory, which instantly made her stiffen, even though her heart was pounding and there was a giddy pulsing in her veins.

'We should be getting back.'

'I thought you were concerned about my handling the boat with too much alcohol in my system.'

'James…'

'I've always liked the way you say my name, in that husky voice of yours.'

'Don't.'

'Come sit next to me and then tell me *don't…*' But he didn't leave her wriggle room, instead fluidly vaulting to his feet and before she could take evasive action. He was there, next to her, his body warm and still slightly damp, smelling of the salty sea and something else...

Ellie's breath hitched in her throat and everything in her body seemed to grind to a halt.

When she dropped her gaze, it was to rest on his hand, loose on his thigh.

She could feel his eyes on her, his attention on her, and the silence pressed down until it was suffocating.

When he stroked the soft underside of her wrist with his finger, she closed her eyes and gritted her teeth together.

'Look at me.'

'I… I can't.'

'Why not?'

Ellie glanced sideways but then she couldn't stop herself from feasting her eyes on him.

So beautiful, so dangerous. Up close with him like this felt like the first taste of forbidden fruit and the wetness of her own arousal made her feel faint.

He trailed his thumb over the fullness of her mouth and, when he very gently eased it between her lips, she gave a soft little moan and sucked on it.

What was she doing? How was she ever going to get back from this?

But she was discovering at speed what that little word *lust* was all about and just how useless common sense was as a weapon with which to ward it off.

His mouth found hers and she melted against him with a sigh of pleasure. She clutched at the tee shirt and her body unconsciously curved towards his, seeking his hardness and his heat. His clothes felt like a barrier between them and she wanted to shove her hands under the tee shirt and tear it off him.

He pushed her back and his kiss deepened and hardened hungrily.

She was barely aware of him scooping her up and carrying her through to one of the four bedrooms, somehow managing to maintain his balance on the gently bobbing boat. The sky could have fallen in and Ellie didn't think she would have noticed, so caught up in the moment was she.

During the course of the day, none of the bedrooms had been used. This one, the master bedroom, was spectacular, with a generous queen-sized bed, and hatches and opening portholes which could allow in natural light.

He deposited her on the bed without bothering to switch on the overhead light, for which she was extremely grateful. Heaven only knew, the cold glare of daylight was just around the corner, and with it would come all those horrifying questions she knew she should be asking herself right now, but for the moment she wanted this so badly…

There was no room for questions as she

watched him peel away the tee shirt and step out of his swimming trunks.

Ellie groaned aloud and resisted the primal urge to touch herself.

Watching you watching me...

James had never been so turned on before in his life. She lay there, clothed but in disarray, her cheeks hectic with colour and those calm grey eyes hot with the same hunger tearing through him. It was like nothing on earth for him.

It *hurt* taking his time. He was so hard for her. He felt the hugeness of himself, and gritted his teeth and remained still for a few seconds, willing himself to take it easy. Just looking at her was enough to make him want to bring himself to a fast climax and there was no way he was going to do that. But those eyes on him, looking at him as he absently played with himself, touching himself…

Was this what playing with fire felt like? Because this *was* playing with fire. Though temptation had never promised to taste sweeter.

He made sure he had protection at hand and then sank onto the mattress alongside her. Here, the slapping of the water against the sides of the boat was more noticeable because the portholes were open.

He kissed her. He teased his tongue into her

mouth and felt her shiver against him. He knew that his hand was not quite as steady as could be expected as he slipped it under the small, stretchy top to find her cotton bra and her small, perfectly shaped breasts. He gently massaged one through the flimsy fabric of her bra.

He'd known she wouldn't wear a swimsuit and she wasn't. What he hadn't expected was how satisfied he'd been that she hadn't frolicked in the sea with the rest of them. He'd had to tear his eyes away from her and it hadn't escaped him that he wasn't the only one. Had she noticed? At any rate, having her remain on deck, dutifully working while they swam, had been just fine with him. He wasn't a jealous guy, but every so often, he'd been honest enough to admit that there was a twinge of something dark that stirred inside him when he caught one of the young guys looking at her.

He baulked at the thought that he might be jealous. He didn't have a jealous bone in his body. To be jealous, you had to invest, and he was over any kind of emotional investment—had been for years.

No. The bottom line was that this sexy creature represented the taste of forbidden fruit, and what could be more succulent?

He eased the bra off her, expertly unclasping it from behind, and groaned as he settled his hand on her bare breast. He raised himself over her, staring down, taking deep breaths as he pulled off the top and bra.

Her skin was soft and smooth, her breasts small and pert, tipped with glorious, pink, circular discs begging to be licked.

But not yet. First he wanted to savour just the stunning sight of her. See all of her…

He undid the sarong with shaking hands. Underneath she had on a pair of tight shorts, red to match the colours in the sarong, and underneath that her panties.

A voyage of discovery. Heady, sexy, mind-blowing. He'd returned to an adolescent place where he was no longer in control of his reactions. He should have been disconcerted, but instead it was a turn-on. Like taking a white-water ride.

Ellie blossomed under that fierce, appreciative gaze. His nakedness was intensely erotic. When he had clothes on, his good looks were on the killer scale. With him naked, words failed her.

She had never lain like this before, with a man's eyes hungry on her naked body. Her one boyfriend, the guy who should have been her soul mate, because they had known one another for a couple of years before going out, had been a disappointment. It had been a classic case of friends who should never have strayed from the straight and narrow. They had parted company without any bad feelings at all. They followed one another on social media, offering appropriate congratulations as necessary at life's small triumphs, but all that she had taken from it was the firm conviction that, when it came to the physical, she was sorely lacking.

Ben had been pleasant, kind and good-looking. Theoretically, it should have been good between them. Shouldn't it? So this intense reaction now was something she was ill-prepared for and she could feel it sweeping her along with the ferocity of a tidal wave.

The first touch made her moan out loud and she squirmed as he settled over her and began exploring her breasts with his tongue, with his mouth, with his hands.

Not even in her wildest imaginings had anything felt so good. He suckled on her nipples, drawing them into his mouth while he stroked the soft flesh of her inner thigh. He licked a sensuous path between her breasts and circled her belly button with his finger at the same time. When she squirmed to touch him, he gently propelled her back to tell her that he wanted her to feel like she'd never felt before.

'But…' she protested helplessly and he smiled.

'Don't worry. I'm not a saint. I want you

touching me badly and we have all night to indulge… I'm happy to wait.'

'All night?' She'd almost forgotten that they were still on the yacht.

'I have this boat for as long as I want it.'

Ellie sighed. She wriggled as he continued to touch her, stroking her stomach and circling her nipples with his finger. Then his mouth replaced his finger, and she gasped and breathed in sharply as he traced a sensuous path down her stomach with his tongue, inching lower, then parting her thighs with his hands so that she was open to him.

Then he kissed her between her legs, a gentle kiss, blowing softly before inserting his tongue into her wetness. Her instinct at this shocking show of intimacy was to snap her legs together. This was a place to which she had never gone before and an experience she had never had. However, he kept them open and she sank into the most shatteringly exquisite sensations she had ever had.

She squirmed against his questing tongue and groaned uncontrollably as it delved deeper into her, finding the pulsing beat of her clitoris and staying there to tease the swollen bud until she felt the spiral of pleasure soaring out of control. Her orgasm was unstoppable and she arched against his mouth and cried out, her whole body racked with a shuddering, climactic loss of control that blanked everything out of her mind.

Surfacing should have been horribly awkward. Mortification should have been tearing through her as cold reality took grip and made a mockery of her loss of inhibition. Instead, there was no time for searching questions, because now he guided her to pleasing him and, once again, she was lost in the moment and wonderfully *present* for the first time in her life.

Every touch and every sensation exploded in Technicolor. The feel of him and the taste of him as she explored his body the way he had explored hers was an exquisite voyage of discovery, and it felt weirdly *right*, even though a little voice in the back of her mind was telling her that it was anything *but*.

The ripple of muscle under her fingers and the sinewy strength of his body made her giddy with wanting. The sound of his low, urgent groans and the thick shakiness of his voice as he encouraged her where to go, where to touch and how to touch, made her melt.

Swept away on a surge of never-before-felt sensory overload, she only really came back down to earth when at last they lay next to one another on the queen-sized bed, utterly spent. Shyly, she reached for the sheet, but he flipped onto his side to look at her and gently steered her away from covering herself.

'You have an amazing body,' he murmured, sliding one hand along her waist to rest on her hip.

'James…'

'I know exactly what you're going to say.'

'Do you?' She angled herself so that they were facing one another. The silvery light filtering into the cabin made the shadows dance around them and on their faces, but she could see that his eyes were both serious and ever so mildly amused.

His casualness relaxed her. She wasn't sure what she had been expecting post coitus. Maybe horror and embarrassment from him at what had taken place between them. She had steeled herself to deal with his recriminations as well as her own but there was a smile tugging the corners of his mouth.

'You're going to remind me that I'm your boss and that what we just did was the worst thing we could have done…'

'Isn't it?'

'We are two adults who gave in to the chemistry between us. I don't make a habit of sleeping with my employees…in fact, I have *never* been tempted to do anything of that sort…but we slept together and I'm not going to beat myself up over it. Are you?'

'I'd planned on doing that, now that you mention it.'

He laughed and stroked her cheek. 'There's that sense of humour again…don't beat yourself up, Ellie.'

'It's easy for you to say. I don't do this sort of thing.'

'Never?'

'I… Life has always been a serious business for me,' she admitted. 'I've had one boyfriend, but flings? Hopping in and out of bed with strangers? That life belongs to some other girl…'

'We're not strangers to one another.'

'I know but…'

'Shh.' He rested one finger against her lips, silencing her. 'Did you enjoy what we just did? Did you enjoy making love with me?'

His words invoked a rush of heady pleasure and she briefly closed her eyes and breathed in deeply. There was no way she could lie, and she liked his honesty. She nodded, and he laughed softly and told her that she'd have to speak up because he didn't quite catch what she was saying.

'I enjoyed it.' Ellie glared at him, then smiled and tentatively outlined his mouth with her finger.

'So did I. Plenty. Think we should go there again?'

'We can't!' Her grey eyes were confused when

they met his. 'How can we? We would never be able to work alongside one another again. It would spoil the relationship we have, and I enjoy my job too much to risk losing it.'

'Don't you think it would be worse if we cut it short now?'

'What do you mean?'

'Think about it, Ellie. We turn our backs on one another and agree to move forward and put this down to a one-off escapade...'

'Yes, exactly!' But there was already a coldness seeping inside her at the prospect of that, even though she knew it made perfect sense.

'Hold on. I'm not finished quite yet.' He sifted his fingers through her hair, twirling a silky strand into a ringlet and then letting it fall, slippery straight again. 'We take that road and how does that play out for us working together, with all that pent-up chemistry still sizzling between us? It would be impossible to relax back into anything approaching a decent working relationship.

'There would also be the danger of everyone eventually sussing that something was going on between us. Some of those employees of mine can trace the scent of something off with the accuracy of a bloodhound. They would see the change between us, and it wouldn't take long for them to put two and two together. And how do you think you would be able to deal with that?'

Ellie could feel tears pricking behind her eyelids but she had no one but herself to blame for this situation. She could have pushed him away. He wouldn't have persisted. Instead, she had allowed curiosity through the front door so that it could kill the proverbial cat.

'You're firing me,' she said bluntly, swinging back and resting one arm across her face.

'Don't be ridiculous. Of course I'm not firing you, Ellie! Why would I do that when you're the best PA I've ever had? Probably the only person on the planet who can put up with me!'

'Then what?' She sneaked a glance at him from under her lashes and her breath caught in her throat as their eyes collided.

'I'm saying we give in to this thing between us…let it run its course as it will. We're here, far away from prying eyes. Let's enjoy this, and trust me, by the time I'm back in London after my brother's wedding this will be nothing more than a pleasant memory which we will be more than happy to relegate to the history books. We'll be able to face one another as we always have done and, if there's an extra added facet to our relationship, then it won't interfere with anything. In fact, it might make what we have even better…'

Ellie's brain seemed to get stuck on the bit about relegating it to the history books, but she swept past that discomfort, because he was right. This was lust, and lust never lasted.

He was also right when he said that to end this prematurely would make things impossible between them because there would be that charge, that *electricity*, waiting to be snuffed out.

Another week here… She thought about this, about the freedom to touch him when she wanted, and she felt faint.

She would return to London ahead of him. He would fly to Hawaii shortly after she left. He had already mentioned drumming up some business there that could dovetail with the Barbados deal. He would have time to explore that before the wedding and then, by the time he was finally back in London, she would be back to her normal self.

She almost laughed because she felt that, once those prim suits were back in place, she would revert to the person she had always been. Her personality was way too ingrained for it to be thrown off-course by a week of giddy passion.

'Maybe…' she whispered, looking down at unknown depths beneath her feet, poised to take a leap. 'Maybe you're right…'

CHAPTER SIX

Ellie looked over the top of her book towards the horizon and James, now just a little dot moving in the blue, blue sea in an apparent bid to reach that invisible point.

Pure bliss.

At a little after four in the afternoon, the sun was still beating down, as golden as honey. The families had started drifting off, but even when the beach had been full, at midday, Ellie and James had still managed to secure a private, quiet spot on the never-ending stretch of powder-white sand. There they had settled down with their lavish picnic, prepared with care by the chefs at the hotel.

What lay round the corner was something she had put on hold, a bridge to be crossed when the time came, and that time wasn't now. What lay round the corner was a little thing called *reality*.

She hadn't been born yesterday. They were in a bubble. In this bubble James was charmed by the novelty of being with a woman who wasn't high maintenance, who didn't come with myriad potential complications and who was fundamentally sensible enough to walk away without kicking up a fuss—unlike his ex. But those were details she had set aside for *tomorrow.*

Now was…*this*. A beach, a book, the sun and that disappearing dot… James… *Her lover...*

Yes, the days were going by, but slowly. This was day three and it felt as though time was standing still, everything moving with a casual lack of urgency. This was an island where no one saw the need to rush, and it was incredible how quickly both of them had adapted. The deal was just about there, going through the last-stage formalities where lawyers swarmed all over documents like flies. But there was no sense of speed because the guys all took the stance of, 'Hey, it's going to happen, so why the rush? Enjoy the island first!'

So plans had changed accordingly, with James's trip to Hawaii being put back by several days to accommodate their easy going business partners. He would be cutting it a bit fine, but he would still have time to spare before the wedding.

Ellie had been overjoyed, but she had concealed it well, because he had made it very clear that this was all about living for the moment and that was a concept she was eager to embrace. 'Living for the moment' didn't involve any dangerous, unstable waters, any currents that could drag her under.

'You understand me,' he had told her only the day before as they had lain on the deck of the Catamaran, out in the middle of the deep blue sea, with nothing on and pleasurably sated from making love.

The compliment had been a double-edged sword, though, because he had continued, smiling, lying on one side so that he could tease her nipple with a finger. 'You know I don't believe in permanence so there's no chance you would ever get the wrong idea about this, about what we have.'

He'd been lying back, squinting at the azure sky for a few seconds, his hands behind his head. 'I made a mistake with Naomi,' he had mused. 'I believed her when she told me that she was into her career, that she was on the same page as I was, that what we had was fun.'

When he'd looked at her again, his dark blue eyes had been serious and yet lazily appreciative. 'You and I…' he'd grinned crookedly '…have been together long enough for you to know just where I stand on that subject.'

So, yes, Ellie knew just what the limits of this relationship were. She had realised very quickly that a display of *anything* that might be interpreted as her looking for more than what was on the table would be a very bad idea indeed.

But was she looking for anything more than what was on the table? She told herself not, but was she being completely truthful?

It was a question that had lodged itself at the back of her mind and exploring that would open a Pandora's box which she might find impossible to shut once the lid had been lifted.

She knew that as instinctively as she knew that he would be able to put this brief distraction behind him without any difficulty. He knew how to compartmentalise. It was what made it impossible for his emotions to take the lead. In so many ways, he had imparted that information to her without her even really realising it. In so many ways, his values were the polar opposite of hers…so wasn't that protection enough against anything…dangerous?

When they were with their business contacts, James was all business. He didn't try and pretend that there was nothing going on between them, but she knew that his focus was elsewhere, on the deal finally waiting to be sealed, with signatures on all the right lines. Work was his priority and all else was pushed into the background next to it.

It was why he could operate a constantly revolving door situation with the women he dated. He gave them one hundred percent of his undivided attention while the romance was running hot, but the second he began walking away was the second they became part and parcel of his past.

She was in a different category, because she would still be working with him, but she knew that the same principle would be applied. Once back in London, she would revert to being his PA, and if there was an added dimension to their relationship then that was something he would find amusing but certainly not a distraction.

And for her that worked…*didn't it?*

Like he'd said, she thought, with just the faintest stirrings of unease as that distant dot began to head back to shore, once this was out of their system normality would return. The electricity would fizzle out. That was how it had always been for him and for her…

She might have had next to no experience but she certainly knew what her head told her. He fundamentally wasn't her type, which meant that what she felt was purely lust, and everyone knew that lust and longevity were not things that went hand in hand. Lust wore thin very quickly. The fact that he would set the example by switching off would help their working relationship.

She would simply follow his lead and it would be fine.

Of course it would!

She sat up, drawing her knees to her chest, watching as he swam back to shore. Next to her was the camera he had bought at huge cost two days ago. She would never have guessed that he was a spectacularly adventurous photographer, but it was a hobby that somehow fitted his unpredictable, highly creative yet incredibly driven personality.

It also gave an insight into someone who enjoyed a sense of solitude, which no one would ever have guessed, given the charming, extrovert nature of his personality. Those glimpses of his complexities had fired up her curiosity and imagination, but she knew that that too was a dangerous response, because it sucked her in, dismantling the necessary distance she was trying to maintain between them.

But, good heavens, keeping him at arm's length was tough to maintain when he made her body soar, her mouth run dry and scrambled her brain so that thinking straight felt like an effort demanding huge will power.

She watched as he stood up, shook the water off, raked his fingers through his hair and began walking towards her, every movement poetry in action.

Behind him, the backdrop of crystalline, azure water and the deepening blue of the late-afternoon sky was so picture-perfect that she wanted to grab the camera and capture it before it was lost to time and memory.

His wet swimming trunks clung to his muscular thighs and dipped down below his belly button, perfectly emphasising his six pack. Hiding behind her sunglasses, Ellie watched, mesmerised by his sheer animal beauty.

He was grinning when he stopped in front of her and held out his hand for her to grab.

'I can't see the expression on your face when you're hiding behind those things,' he teased. 'But I'm hoping that it's unfettered joy at the thought of us heading back to the bedroom...'

Ellie shielded her face and allowed herself to be pulled to her feet.

The modest black swimsuit she had brought with her had been replaced with a racier number in the sort of bright colours she would previously have avoided.

Shopping for non-essentials, that enjoyable leisure activity beloved by most twenty-somethings, was something she'd had neither the time nor the inclination to indulge. Here in this lazy heat, and basking in the open appreciation of the least suitable guy on the planet, she had discovered that it was something she rather enjoyed.

She glanced down at his long fingers entwined with hers and shivered, because there was something so intimate about the simple gesture. It was as though they were two lovers holding hands, maybe with a future stretching out in front of them.

She quickly whipped her straying thoughts away from any such cosy notion. There was no 'maybe' future for them on any romantic level. What they had was the here and now, and that was a good thing, because he could break a girl's heart. *Her heart, were she to be foolish enough to give it to him.*

'I forgot to mention,' he said, scooping up the remains of their picnic and stuffing it all into the basket provided by the hotel. 'I had a text from Izzy.'

'Your sister?' Ellie had met Izzy in passing a couple of times and had liked what she had seen. She was a stunning blonde girl who clearly adored her slightly older brother.

'She doesn't want to ruin Max and Mia's big day, but she said she couldn't keep the secret to herself any longer…'

'She's getting married?'

'To the guy of her dreams, it would seem,' James drawled, eyebrows raised with amusement. 'It seems my family are falling like ninepins.'

'Are they waiting for it to be your turn next?'

Ellie said lightly. Staring straight ahead, with swaying coconut trees on one side and the gently rolling blue water on the other, her bare feet leaving footprints on the powdery, pale sand, she wondered what it would feel like to have the love of the guy holding her hand.

'Not if they're in their right minds,' he returned wryly.

'I've only met your brother once, but he didn't strike me as the sort who was keen to walk down the aisle…' She remembered a striking, dark-haired guy with scarily forbidding features, as tough as James, but without the easy charm that made his brother so accessible.

'I hope this isn't the sound of you thinking that I'm the sort of guy to be seduced by family peer pressure…'

His voice was still teasing but there was an undercurrent of coolness running through it that set off a warning bell in Ellie's head.

'I hope you're not,' she returned swiftly, and she felt his sidelong glance, although he didn't break stride.

'Intriguing remark. Want to expand?'

Ellie felt the hot tingle of perspiration on her face. This was a forceful reminder of the limits of what they had, and he was reminding her that that was something she would do well not to forget.

Pride stiffened her. The last thing she needed was for him to get the idea that she was somehow morphing into one of those women who ended up hanging onto his every word, weeping, wailing and falling apart when he decided that it was time to move on.

He laid down parameters. Well, she, for one, would be following them!

'You don't have to worry that I would ever get the wrong idea about...*this*...' she said, with an equal amount of coolness in her voice. 'I won't. What we have stays here, and that suits me very well, not just because anything else would interfere with my working relationship with you but because you're the last kind of guy I would go for. In fact, I would say that you've done me a favour...'

'How so?'

'You've reminded me that I'm still young,' Ellie told him, and that was the truth. 'That there are guys out there, and that falling in love is still something that is waiting for me. You've given me back my confidence.'

'I'm very glad to be of service,' James murmured.

Everything she had just said should be exactly what he wanted to hear because it all made sense.

For a second, when she'd hinted that he might

be inclined to follow in his siblings' footsteps, he had thought she might be dropping hints.

Nothing had given him any suspicion that she might be following in Naomi's footsteps, tempted to barge past the Keep Out signs, refusing to give up even after the door had been slammed shut, but could he be sure? She remained as professional as she always was when they were in the company of their business partners, even fractionally moving off if he got too close.

To his surprise, he found her evasive measures irritating. He had perversely wanted to touch her, to remind their potential business partners that she was his. He hadn't. Possessiveness was something he personally had no time for as a trait and, if fleetingly he had wanted to stake his claim, then that had to do with a perfectly gentlemanly desire to protect her from any developing situations she might not have been able to handle. The guys were exuberant and open in their appreciation of what they saw.

Good job the deal was practically done.

A few more days here and they would go their separate ways and, when they next met, normality would once again be resumed.

It was exactly what he wanted, and the fact that she had reassured him that she wasn't about to get any ideas about where this was going should have made him feel better than it did.

Disgruntled, he wondered whether it would be appropriate to point out that not many men liked seeing themselves as a trial run for other guys!

That was the only reason her remarks had made him feel edgy. Truth was, he had timelines when it came to women, and she was no different, even though she might have known him better than most. Possibly better than anyone else did. Inevitable, given that she worked for him and saw him more than most men saw their wives.

What they had would run its course. Every involvement with every woman always ran its course in the end. It was the way he liked it. Nothing deep and so no messy, painful aftermath. So why the hell was he ever so slightly irked at what she'd just said?

He dropped her hand and moved a little away, creating necessary distance between them, searching for his self-control, wondering whether the sun and forty minutes worth of swimming in open ocean had done something to him—made him a bit light-headed, made him think that she'd got under his skin a little too much for his liking.

'I've completed the last bits of paperwork for the deal here.' Ellie noted the way he had stopped holding hands and stepped just fractionally away.

Did he think that he had to further remind her that this meant nothing to him but a bit of fun?

Had she somehow communicated something to him...done something to make him think otherwise...?

Anxiously, Ellie tried to think back. The mere fact that she felt she might have somehow signalled to him that she was in deeper than she'd ever expected, despite the very sensible mantras she kept repeating to herself, sent a chill of apprehension racing up and down her spine.

Bring it back to work...

In the thick, suddenly uncomfortable silence, she chatted about everything she had managed to get through earlier while he had been in front of his laptop. Legal technicalities had been ironed out! Patents sorted! Signatures were awaited but she didn't foresee any problems…

Eventually, her voice tapered off and she stared straight ahead. For the first time she was blind to the exotic beauty of their surroundings, to the hum of distant insects, the sound of the lapping ocean, the stunning riot of colour of all the flowers, the people and the infectious sound of laughter.

She felt the loss of his touch like a physical

blow, and that scared her, making her doubly determined to keep her feelings under wraps.

Their dedicated chauffeur was waiting to take them back to the hotel. She slid into the back seat and closed her eyes for a few seconds, enjoying the cool air-conditioning after the scorching heat outside.

What was going on? Was this the prelude to the goodbye speech? Only now that it was imminent did she realise how much she had been looking forward to really enjoying the last few days with him.

Did that make her seem clingy? The very thought was mortifying. She thought of poor Naomi and felt a twinge of intense sympathy.

She clasped her hands together on her lap and stared through the tinted windows, wondering what line of conversation to take to break the increasingly uncomfortable silence between them.

'You've gone quiet on me,' James murmured. Ellie slid her gaze across and breathed a mental sigh of relief because the sudden coolness between them had filled her with horror, disproportionately so.

'Have I? I thought I'd been talking quite a bit about closing this deal we've come here to do.'

'Less work and more play…'

'If you say so…you're the boss, after all…' He tugged gently and she shuffled closer to him.

He closed the privacy partition, separating them from their driver, and tilted her face to his.

'I am,' he agreed, tracking the outline of her mouth with his finger and sending a thousand little electrical impulses reverberating through her body. 'I've spent the whole day wanting to touch you. In fact, if it weren't for the fact that we'll be at the hotel in under twenty minutes, I would be doing a lot more than I'm doing now…'

'Really?' Ellie queried huskily. 'Like what?'

'I'd quite like to pay some attention to your breasts… Have I mentioned that you have beautiful ones?'

'James, stop!' But she was laughing as her whole body went up in flames at his evocative words and the searing hunger in his dark eyes.

'Tell me I'm not turning you on…'

'Maybe you are.'

'Just *maybe*? Maybe you'll get a little more turned on if I tell you that I'm looking forward to taking that bikini off you very, very slowly and then, once I've devoted sufficient attention to your breasts, I intend to get between your legs and taste you down there until you're begging me not to stop…'

'Shh…'

'Are you wet for me yet?'

'You know I am.'

'Would you like to come against my mouth? I know you enjoy that…'

'Not as much as I enjoy feeling you inside me.' Looking at herself from a distance, looking at the woman now saying what she had just said, Ellie could scarcely believe her ears. She had never thought she could be so uninhibited and she had to acknowledge that that had been his great gift to her.

She had opened up with him, against all odds, and she had blossomed in ways she could never have imagined.

She was in such desperate need of being touched, after that hot conversation in the back of the car, that she practically leapt out of her seat before the driver had had a chance to pull to a stop.

And James was in as much of a hurry as she was.

They were holding hands, and neither of them had expected to be greeted by a woman. Indeed, they barely realised that they were on a collision course with the towering blonde until she was suddenly *there*, right in front of them, her expression more shock than fury.

James gathered himself at speed and stood back, expression closed, concealing his shock as he looked at his ex for a few stunned seconds.

'Naomi. What the hell are you doing here?'

'I came…to see whether we could patch things up. I know you never answered my texts but… I know how proud you are…' She was talking to James. She was staring at Ellie. Her cool, assessing eyes glittered as hard as diamonds.

'I told you it was over.' His voice was tight and controlled.

He had managed to pull them all to one side. Ellie was hardly aware of being manoeuvred out of the main stream of traffic along with Naomi, who was wearing the briefest of shorts, the tiniest of cropped tops and carrying a holdall bearing a well-known logo.

'So what's going on between the two of you?'

Her voice had risen. Ellie could feel curious eyes on them. Hardly surprising, given the fact that Naomi was clearly a supermodel, James was clearly incredibly important and incredibly wealthy and the altercation between them was clearly going south.

A cabaret of sorts was about to commence and who wouldn't be interested in taking a ringside to witness the event?

She thought of Naomi kicking off at the office in her absence and wondered whether a repeat performance was on the cards, this time with a far more judgemental audience.

'This was supposed to be *our* holiday, James! I even *chose this hotel*!'

'I am *not* going to get into this with you again, Naomi. This was not a trip for you to make. I don't want a scene in a public place but I'm warning you—if you don't leave, I'll have no option but to call the manager to have you discreetly escorted out of the hotel.'

'You can't do that! This is a public place! Besides, you wouldn't *dare* risk a scene!'

'Want to try me?'

'Were you involved with your little secretary before we broke up, James?'

Everything in Ellie wanted to rage against the sweeping insult behind that accusation, but tact made her hold back the words begging to be delivered.

She was on the periphery of this, and besides, whatever the rights or wrongs of Naomi showing up on the island in the hope that her physical charms might achieve what texts and phone calls presumably hadn't, Ellie felt a twinge of sympathy for the other woman.

She was uneasily aware of just how effortlessly you could get blinded to the reality of a situation. James was just so persuasive, so charming, so incredibly dynamic, sharp, clever and unexpectedly thoughtful in ways you could never have predicted.

Just as well she knew the parameters of this game being played, but even so…

Naomi had wanted more. Without those parameters really in place, was it any wonder she had been tempted to show up here…?

'Okay. I think I've had enough of this.' He looked around, searching for one of the members of staff.

Ellie stepped in to say quietly, 'That's insulting to James and it's insulting to me, what you're inferring.'

'Well, it's obvious that you two are an item,' Naomi bit back without hesitating. 'It's obvious you're *all loved up*. Do you honestly think you're going to get anywhere with him when *I* couldn't?'

Out of the corner of her eye, Ellie could see the worried face of the hotel manager as he scuttled at pace across the marble foyer.

'You won't!' Naomi leaned in to Ellie.

'You don't understand…' Ellie began, distraught at what was happening, and keen to eliminate herself from a scenario in which she didn't feel she truly belonged.

How dared this perfect stranger think that she, Ellie, was so lacking in principles that she would have hopped into bed with her boss while he was seeing another woman?

Yet, she *had* hopped into bed with him, hadn't she? And the time lag between Ellie doing that and him breaking up with the stupendously beautiful blonde looking at her with ice-cold eyes *had* been shamelessly brief, hadn't it?

So Naomi had flown over here, desperate to effect a reconciliation…

And Ellie? Was clinging to these last few days just as desperate—even if her desperation was hidden behind a veneer of self-control and nonchalant acceptance of the ground rules laid down?

When she thought of their relationship coming to an end, to returning to London where she would plaster a bright, beaming smile on her face and pretend nothing had happened, there was a feeling of terrifying *emptiness* underneath all the bracing assumptions that this was something that would fade in no time at all.

How different was she really from the woman who had crossed the Atlantic to reconnect with a guy who no longer wanted her? How vulnerable would *she* find herself when things resumed between them professionally, with this brief interlude relegated to the history books?

Had anything in her life prepared her for this? No. Too many years living a sheltered life had allowed James, with his larger-than-life personality, to roar through her with the force of an all-consuming tidal wave, battering down the door she had spent so many years keeping firmly shut between them.

Suddenly exposed to thoughts she had managed to wilfully avoid, Ellie felt her heart begin to race.

Low, urgent words were being exchanged between James and Naomi, but it was all just background noise, eclipsed by a weird thundering in her ears and a sickening realisation that she had managed to lose all control over what was happening in her life.

Having been immersed in her thoughts, she resurfaced to Naomi hissing under her breath that she would be sorry.

Sorry for what?

She looked at James in confusion, feeling as though she'd fallen asleep during the middle of a play only to wake up to an ending that made no sense.

'James may have told you that he's serious about you, but he's not. Word to the wise: don't get your hopes up. *There won't be a wedding ring on that finger any time soon!*'

She spun on her heels, sweeping past the hotel manager who had halted in his tracks at some point, no doubt having been given an invisible signal by James. Eyes followed her, avidly curious. One or two phones were recording the whole episode but Ellie had too much on her mind to pay a blind bit of notice to any of that.

Instead, she scrambled behind James as he

summoned the lift with a thunderous expression which he couldn't quite manage to conceal.

As with the snapping smartphones, Ellie ignored the thunderous expression and said bluntly, just as soon as the doors had snapped shut behind them, 'What did she mean by that?'

'By what?'

'Fingers and wedding rings! Did you tell her that we were some kind of *item*?'

'It would have been difficult for her to have escaped that conclusion.'

'No, it would have been very easy to have set her straight!'

The lift doors pinged open and she hurried after him, eager to have the privacy of a room with no chance of wagging ears or eyes on stalks.

'We were holding hands when we entered the lobby,' he reminded her with a level of calm that got on her nerves. 'You were flushed with wanting me. We couldn't wait to get back to the bedroom. A fool with poor eyesight would have been able to put two and two together.'

He was stripping off as he spoke, prowling the elegant sitting area that adjoined the massive bedroom.

All that startling masculine beauty. It had got right to her, demolished her defences, but she refused to allow it to leave her helpless. She wasn't going to drift along until things fizzled out between them in a few days' time.

In some way, Naomi's appearance had put things into miserable perspective, and if she didn't take hold of the reins now then when would she?

'So now she thinks that this is serious? Now she thinks that you broke up with her so that you could bring me here to take her place?'

'Do either of us care what Naomi thinks?'

His eyes were cool, already distant. Ellie wondered whether, down the line, he would care what *she* thought. No chance. He was impervious to emotion, which was why it was so easy for him to take what he wanted when it came to women and then discard them when they began to bore him.

'I care,' Ellie said quietly. '*I* care, James. I'm not like you. I can't just do whatever I want to do and to heck what other people think.'

He flushed darkly and raked his fingers through his hair. He'd stripped off the shirt, unbuttoning the shorts that hung low on lean hips. She had to look away so that her body didn't begin misbehaving. With an unconscious gesture of self-defence, she hugged herself and stared at him, not having moved from the door, having remained standing while he had powered into the room.

'Who says we aren't an item?'

'You let her think that this was serious, and it's not, and I know why you did that. You did it because you wanted to get rid of her and that was the most efficient way of doing it.'

'She was going to believe what she wanted to believe,' James countered, but he hadn't breached the distance between them, and the air shimmered with antagonism.

'I think we need to call it day.'

'Oh, for God's sake, Ellie. Isn't that something of an overreaction? Why? Because an ex huffed and puffed and thought she could blow the house down?'

Because I think I'm falling in love with you.

It was a shattering realisation, one that had crept up and ambushed her when she hadn't been looking. She *should* have been looking. Instead, she had been busily telling herself that she couldn't possibly fall for him because she was *too sensible*. As if being sensible made her invincible.

She breathed in deeply, taking her time to think, knowing that hysteria on any level just wasn't going to work.

'Because I stepped back, had a good, long look at myself and I didn't like what I saw.'

'Which was what?'

Which was a complete fool with cotton wool for a brain.

'I wasn't raised to have flings. It's not what I do, and it's especially horrible to know that someone might actually think I'm the kind of person who doesn't mind sleeping around with some guy who's involved with someone else. I was brought up with a lot of principles, and I guess I thought I could dump them for a while, but I was wrong. I can't. We could carry on with what we have but, now that I've come to my senses, it would be hard for me to return to where we were…'

She sighed and looked away. She wished she could read what he was thinking but, for a guy who was apparently so open, he was adept when it came to revealing only what he wanted to reveal. Right now, she had no idea what was going through his head.

'In that case,' he said coolly, 'you're probably right. I'm not looking for involvement, Ellie. Not me. Never will be.'

A dagger had just shot through her heart but she only had herself to blame. She nodded and managed a smile. 'I'll move myself back to my bedroom…'

And what happens next?

He answered that unspoken question without

her having to try and find a subtle way of asking it.

'I anticipate,' he drawled, 'that all signatures will be in place tomorrow. There's no more schmoozing to be done. The deal will have been done. To avoid any potential awkwardness, you are free to arrange a flight back for yourself, and I will see you when I return to London in a couple of weeks.' He inclined his head to one side and gave her a half mocking salute. 'That suit you?'

'Yes.' Ellie nodded, her face as blank as his. 'That would be for the best…'

CHAPTER SEVEN

JAMES GAZED OUT from the balcony of his suite at a view that was incomparable.

Sprawled on the hand-made bamboo chair, long legs stretched out on the matching footstool and hands folded behind his head, he let his eyes feast on a tapestry of navy blue sea and a sky that was ablaze with all the vibrant colours of sunset. Russet and burnt orange against a backdrop of deepest indigo and midnight-blue. No painter could have captured the natural beauty.

However, as he nursed a rum, the only persistent image in his head was that of his recently departed personal assistant.

For the first time since they had touched down on the island, his bed was empty. In a fitful sleep, he had rolled onto his side at a little after three in the morning, automatically reaching out for her warmth, but had jerked awake, uncomfortable at the thought that he didn't care for the sudden emptiness of his sleeping arrangements.

Since when had he had a problem sleeping on his own? Indeed, that was something he had always actively encouraged. It was rare for any woman to occupy his bed overnight, and certainly never for nights on end, as though some kind of habit was being nurtured.

He had been interested to see how breakfast together would go, following what he still considered to be an overly dramatic and premature ending to what they had going on. He'd imagined that he might have to deal with her embarrassment.

Understandable.

She lacked his considerable experience in these matters. In fact, when he thought about her, which he had done for most of the night, it was to conclude that she was strangely innocent and touchingly disingenuous, despite the outward image of a cool, controlled and utterly unflappable professional.

It tickled him pink to think that he was the one-in-a-million guy who had seen right into that very private part of her.

So he had been surprised and a little disgruntled, several hours earlier, when he had sat down to breakfast with a woman who was once again metaphorically dressed in her London work uniform.

Every time he had tried to steer the conversation in a more personal direction, she had blanked over and looked at him with polite, ever so amused grey eyes and then promptly returned the conversation right back to work. Deals that were brewing on the side lines… An email from a company he had casually approached six months previously that was now interested in doing business with him… The sudden absence of one of the CEOs whose mother had been rushed to hospital following a car accident…

She had been thoroughly and admirably in control, and *naturally* he had been immensely grateful to be spared the awkwardness of having to get things back on track in preparation for a resumption of their normal working relationship.

He had reminded himself of the continuing nightmare of the ex who couldn't go away. Another lingering ex was the last thing he needed.

Still… Was there any reason for her politely but firmly to decline his suggestion that he accompany her to the airport?

'Good Lord! That's very sweet of you but of course I don't want you coming with me to the airport!' She had knocked back his offer with incredulous laughter and then followed up by wryly informing him that she was perfectly capable of checking in at an airport, even if it *had* been ages since she'd had a chance to go abroad before this.

He had gritted his teeth and smiled when she had earnestly thanked him then for the opportunity to visit such a wonderful island. And when he had tilted his head to the side and asked her whether that was all she wanted to thank him for, she hadn't been in the slightest bit coy.

'Oh, the sex was lovely,' she had said warmly, but her eyes had glazed over, and it had been perfectly clear that the *lovely sex* was something she was already in the process of putting behind her.

Who was he to complain? She'd made it easy for him. She had pulled back from dwelling on the fact that she *didn't do casual*, saving him the necessity of gently reminding her that emotional relationships were a beast he steered clear of.

He drained his glass. It was a little after six and he would spend the remainder of the evening working. He'd signed off on the deal he had come to finalise, and in the blink of an eye he would be boarding a plane for Hawaii, no doubt in the mood for some distraction.

Dwelling was a much-overrated pastime. There would be no time to *dwell* when he was working by day and playing by night. It was a tried and tested formula that had always stood him in good stead. It had worked when his parents had died, and it had worked in the aftermath of his juvenile crush on a woman who had only been good for warming his bed. It would damn well work now.

He stood up, stretched and absently appreciated the rapidly sinking ball of fire disappearing over the horizon. Give it three days and he would probably be hard pressed to remember just how intense the past few days on this island had been…

Ellie gazed at her mobile phone, which had not stopped ringing for the past eight hours.

The trip back had been uneventful enough, and she had almost managed to convince herself that putting distance between them would work wonders when it came to clearing her head.

She'd fallen hook, line and sinker for her boss, and so of course it was going to be a towering mountain to climb for that brief liaison to be erased from her memory bank, but erased it would be. She had no choice in the matter, at least not until she managed to find another job that paid as well.

She had managed to get through the nightmare of their last breakfast together in one piece. Her jaw had ached from the discomfort of the phoney smile she had plastered to her face, but she had got through it, and that was the main thing.

It had been a pointer that overcoming this suffocating misery was achievable.

She landed at Gatwick Airport and took a taxi back to her flat. The idea of trudging on public transport seemed way too depressing and arduous.

She knew that one of the things she would have to become accustomed to was going to be the drudgery of normal life.

She'd always taken great pride in being the sort of person who wasn't easily impressed by the trappings of wealth. She'd worked with James Stowe and seen first-hand the amount of money he lavished on the women he dated, because she often found the receipts for ludicrously expensive items kicking around on his desk, and had privately smirked at the superficiality of those women who were actually impressed by all that sort of stuff.

And yet, she now found herself swelling their numbers, seduced by the pleasure of all those comforts that went hand in hand with great wealth. She had gazed at the perfect splendour of a pristine beach, dipping into a picnic prepared by a top chef, and she had felt so blissfully happy.

Did that make her superficial? No. Worse than

that, she had to acknowledge that she would have felt just as blissfully happy had they been tucking into chicken and chips eaten out of plastic baskets, because James had been the reason for her happiness.

Nevertheless, she would have to come right back down to earth, and fast. And for the first twenty-four hours, she actually believed that that was on the cards. She unpacked, stuffing her newly acquired clothes to the back of her wardrobe, where she anticipated them spending a few years hibernating before she gave them to a charity shop. She could never entertain the notion of wearing all those brightly coloured items of clothing again, not when they would always remind her of a time that had come and gone in the blink of an eye.

Then she had an early night and tried to plan her return to work the following Monday without a broken heart stamped all over her face. The last thing she felt she could deal with was sheepish, embarrassed, inquisitive looks from concerned colleagues.

Fate had other ideas when it came to giving her a break, and now here she was…

What on earth was she going to do?

The phone had been ringing off the hook. There were two men with cameras outside her house, lounging by a car, smoking and waiting for her to emerge from where she had now been in hiding for the past day.

She felt as if she was suddenly under attack on all sides, and she had no idea what she was going to do.

The first call, from one of her colleagues at work, had alerted her to the fact that she was suddenly in the spotlight and *newsworthy.*

'Hey, girl, what's going on?'

Ellie had heard Trish's sing-song voice but, before she'd been able to fill her in on the successful outcome of her trip to Barbados, she had been pinned to the spot by a series of good-natured questions that had left her reeling.

The second she had hung up, she had found the tabloid headlines on her phone and had watched her whole life begin to unravel with sickening horror.

Of course, Ellie had known that James was the darling of the tabloid press. A billionaire, ridiculously good-looking, and with the gravitas and money that came from the complex and cut-throat world of business.

He was also courteous towards reporters. He always seemed to recognise that they were doing a job and, as long as they didn't go anywhere he didn't want them to go, he was unfailingly co-operative. Hence he graced the covers of magazines and newspapers with predictable regularity because of the transitory nature of his relationships and the high profiles of most of his exes.

But now…

Now *she* was the woman…the one who had finally 'snared the country's most eligible bachelor'… The quiet little secretary who had 'worked her magic from the side lines'… The one who had 'managed to get the ring on her finger and the date set for a walk down the aisle'…

Of course, in a week's time this would all be history, and the reporters would be busily finding someone else to pin to the wall, but for now…

For now, she was trapped in her own house and when she did emerge, which she would have to in the next day or two to return to work, she would have to hope and pray that the furore would have died down.

Usually, Ellie would have taken a deep breath and cheerfully told the lot of them that it was all just a ridiculous mistake. If you ploughed your way through a problem, it was usually the fastest way of dealing with it, but there was now the added complication of her mother.

Every problem seemed to open a door to a new one. She cradled a cup of tea, frantically trying to work out how on earth she was going to deal with the accumulated lot of problems.

Her train of thought was interrupted by the frantic ringing of the doorbell. At six thirty in the evening this was the last thing she wanted and she ignored the piercing summons until her mobile phone began ringing as well, and up popped his number.

James.

Her heart stopped and she sank back against the chair and closed her eyes for a second.

Through all this, she hadn't stopped thinking of him. Would news of this have reached him in Barbados? He only read the broadsheets, but the gossip grapevine that did the rounds at work would surely have reached him?

She reluctantly took the call and braced herself to be upbeat when all she wanted to do was hide away until the whole mess blew over.

'Open the door, Ellie!'

'James…' Her voice petered off.

'Open the door! I'm outside.'

'Outside?'

'Standing on your doorstep, to be precise.'

'I don't want to go outside. There are people there.' She heard the sound of tears in her voice and cleared her throat.

'I've got rid of them.'

'You have?' Relief washed over her, and for the first time in her life she weakly discovered what it felt like to have someone there to have her back and pick up the pieces.

Taking no chances and not stopping to be concerned that she was clad in nothing more than an old tee shirt, a pair of tight leggings and some gaily patterned bedroom slippers, Ellie went to the front door and unlocked it just enough to make sure that he was really there.

He was.

The breath whipped out of her and she stared for a few seconds, drinking him in with such shameless compulsion that she forgot the horror of her current situation.

He was in a pair of dark jeans and a dark polo shirt, with a battered tan bomber jacket hooked over one shoulder. He looked so utterly unfazed that she could only stare, mesmerised.

'Shouldn't you be on your way to Hawaii?'

'Open the door and let me in. I've sent the two reporters on their way, but I can't guarantee they won't be back, and an argument on the doorstep when we're due to be married any day soon is going to send them into a feeding frenzy…'

Ellie promptly undid the chain and fell back as he brushed past her into her tiny hallway before spinning round on his heels to look at her.

'Why didn't you call me?' he demanded, staring at her.

How could he be so controlled? So calm, beautiful and utterly unruffled?

It didn't seem fair. She pulled herself up, stiffened her shoulders and glared at him.

'Call about what?' she asked with cool defiance.

Frozen to the spot by the laser sharpness of his eyes, it was an effort to unglue herself from her rigid position and head towards the kitchen, making sure to circle round him. She felt his eyes on her back as she walked ahead of him and into the small kitchen with its weathered pine table and mismatched, colourful chairs she had bought from a car boot sale a few months ago.

Only a handful of days ago, this man had been her lover, but that was then and this was now and Ellie was not going to let him think that she couldn't cope with what was being thrown at her.

Still…

She was glad that he was here. Somehow, his very presence felt like a guarantee that peace and order would be re-established.

'Can I get you some coffee?'

'Can you stop acting as though I'm a stranger? You should have called to tell me that the paparazzi were camping on your doorstep. How long have they been there? Since that bloody article hit the headlines? I'm guessing you've been bombarded with phone calls as well. It's easy for these people to get hold of a mobile number if certain security measures aren't in place.'

Bombarded with information and swept along by his instant dominance over the situation, Ellie could only subside weakly into one of the chairs, where she proceeded to rest her chin in her hands. She looked at him.

Coffee would have to wait. She felt she needed something a lot stronger. Scotch, maybe. A double. Except, there was none in the house. Her phone buzzed and she looked at it but didn't pick up.

'You have my apologies,' James murmured in a low voice. 'You look as though you could use a drink, and I don't blame you. What have you got?'

'There's a bottle of wine in the fridge…' She wanted to be strong and in charge, because they were no longer involved with one another, but it felt so good for him to take charge that she waited and then sighed with barely concealed relief when a glass of wine was placed in front of her.

'Talk to me.'

'Why are you here?' was what came out of her mouth, and he frowned.

'Did you expect me to read all that nonsense emblazoned across the tabloids and then head off to Hawaii, leaving you to deal with the mess?'

'I'm not your problem.'

'Let's put pride to one side just for the moment,' James said neutrally. 'Have you left the house? Spoken to anyone?'

'No and no.' Ellie sighed. 'I've been avoiding the phone. And it's not just the reporters… it's everyone at work. I…' Tears welled up and she hurriedly looked away, stared at her hands on her lap and breathed in deeply. 'It's pretty awful,' she whispered.

Guilt rammed into him with the force of a runaway train. The look on her face…

He'd got on that plane without any internal debate. He'd read what had been unleashed in the gossip columns on the opposite side of the Atlantic and *not* getting on a plane and heading back hadn't been an option. Not when he'd been furious with his ex and even more furious with himself for putting Ellie in the situation in which she had found herself. *You made the mess and it was up to you to clear it up.*

He raked his fingers through his hair now and had to force himself to remain seated when what he wanted to do was vault upright and stride restlessly through the tiny kitchen, unless he brought his mind back under control.

Naomi. Bloody Naomi. Nothing like a woman scorned. She had taken stock of the situation when she had descended unannounced at the hotel in Barbados. She had seen with her own eyes exactly what was happening, and she had reacted with a vengeance, returning to London and running to the newspapers as fast as she could.

And why? Because her ego had taken a battering and she had known the best way she could get her revenge. He was a commitment-phobe? Then why not dump him in his own worst nightmare, publicly engaged to be married to someone, she must have assumed, who would be the last woman on earth he'd be attracted to long term, given his well-publicised penchant for leggy beauties…

Now Ellie was here. He could see that she could barely keep herself together and he couldn't blame her. So guarded, so incredibly private, and now thrust into the limelight in ways that she would find horrifying.

He thought of her returning to work, braving those first steps in and knowing that the gossip mill would have been working overtime, and he inwardly winced.

No point dwelling on it, he decided. A self-pity fest wasn't going to get either of them anywhere.

'A united front and point-blank denial from both of us will kill this rumour dead,' he promised. ‘I could have contacted people I know in that field and put the record straight, but I had to find out what was going on over here. I also baulk at having to justify anything to anyone,’ he admitted. ‘I’m assuming you know who is behind this?’

Ellie nodded. She didn’t trust herself to speak.

‘I don’t have to tell you that my ex has chosen to wage war on the wrong man.’ His face hardened. ‘She will find out that my influence extends much further than she could ever expect. I suggest we face the press together and laugh this whole thing off. It will be an easy enough job to put the blame where it rightfully belongs—on the shoulders of an ex with an axe to grind.’

‘It’s…it’s not as simple as that.’

James frowned. What could more complex?

‘Have your family…? Has it reached them over there?’

‘Izzy has a fondness for tabloids and all things gossip.’ He half smiled wryly. ‘She probably knew before the print on the paper had time to dry.’

‘And have you…told them anything? Have they been in touch?’

‘I thought it best to say nothing until I had spoken to you.’

This was why she had crossed that line, Ellie thought. It had nothing to do with how he looked, the reach of his wealth and influence or even the fact that he was far and away the most dynamic, intelligent, forward-thinking, downright *fascinating* person she had ever met.

It was because he was a decent guy.

She'd somehow managed to convince herself that the sort of man she would eventually go for would be a stereotype, as though decent guys all came wrapped up in the same packaging. But James Stowe, on the surface just the sort she couldn't possibly fall for, ticked every single box when it came to being one of the good guys. And that, she knew now, was why sleeping with him had felt so *right*.

He might not love her, or even care about her the way she loved and cared about him, but he had still thought to consider her amidst all of this, to hear what she had to say.

'My mother has been in touch with me,' Ellie said flatly. 'Several times.' She sipped the wine and felt the rush of alcohol to her head.

He said nothing but his sudden stillness was telling, as was the way he was looking at her, eyes narrowed thoughtfully, head tilted to one side.

'And?' he prompted softly when she lapsed into awkward silence.

'And she's very excited.'

'Ah…'

'I never thought she indulged in gossip mags, but it seems that that's her secret vice.' Ellie smiled wanly. 'It seems that it's the secret vice of her entire book club.' She sighed and looked at him steadily. 'When she phoned me, I honestly had no idea she would have been phoning to tell me how pleased she was for me.'

'Go on,' he encouraged quietly.

'It was the happiest I'd heard her sound in a long time. In fact, just before I flew over to Barbados, I was actually beginning to worry that she was going to give in to her depression again. It's plagued her over the years and, although the doctor would never confirm in so many words, I think that her depression and all the associated stress had something to do with her strokes. She was pleased that I was going to Barbados... Maybe she doesn't need me as she once did, but underneath it all I still worry that she could so easily slide back down that hill. She called...she called and she was so pleased for me.'

'I see.'

Ellie didn't have to read the expression on his face to know what was going through his head.

He'd banked on a swift explanation to the press, probably a couple of phone calls and a joint statement from them both, shrugging off the whole sorry saga.

Yes, Naomi had exaggerated everything

wildly out of context, but a woman scorned, he would doubtless insinuate, would be capable of any number of things from slashing tyres to fabricating ruinous stories.

He rightfully assumed that, if you gave too much airtime to gossip, you breathed life into it.

But now…

Now, behind that carefully guarded expression, he would be livid and she felt terrible about that.

'I'm afraid that if I laugh it all off my mum will be distraught, even if she did a job of hiding it, and I'm afraid for her health—both mentally and physically.'

'And for good reason, from what you've told me.'

'I'm very sorry about this,' she said in as controlled a voice as she could muster. 'I'll have to… Of course, things will be sorted and the truth told…'

'Well, not entirely the truth.'

'What do you mean?'

'There may have been some colourful exaggeration as to the gravity of our relationship, but we *were* lovers.'

Ellie reddened. Heat coursed through her body, setting every nerve ending alight and rousing a vivid imagination she had spent the past couple of days trying to extinguish.

She squirmed, the breath catching in her throat, and once again she was helplessly aware of the thoughts leaving her head in a rush while her body kicked in with gusto.

'Yes, well, I obviously won't… I mean, that's all over now, so there would be no point… The fact is that I wanted to go and see Mum so that I could explain everything face to face.' She took a deep breath and exhaled slowly. 'I know this must be just awful for you,' she said quietly. 'If you would wait just a bit before you say anything to the press, then I would be so grateful. Mum would be so confused if she were to be let down by reading another gaudy headline.' She sighed. 'I can't bear to imagine what's going through her head now. What must she think of me?'

'Why would she think anything differently of you?'

'She knows that this…this *person* who went off and had some fling with her boss on a tropical island isn't the girl she brought up. If you knew my mother, you'd understand what I'm saying.'

She had never been a risk taker. She had been brought up in a loving and careful way. You could never have a guarantee when it came to matters of the heart, but with James there was only ever going to be one outcome. Sleeping with her boss had been like jumping from an aeroplane without a parachute. In a life where Ellie had had to deal with pain, she had foolishly courted yet more of it without meaning to, and now this horribly contorted situation had come down to this—a situation where it wasn't just *she* who was affected.

James looked at that soft, vulnerable face, a face she had always been so careful to conceal, and something twisted painfully inside him.

She would suddenly have found herself besieged by slings and arrows on every front. He marvelled that, not only had she not jumped on the phone and demanded he sort things out, but she was here, clearly upset and yet still trying hard to put a brave face on it.

'You could be wrong.'

'I'm not. Trust me.' She smiled wanly. 'I was an only child. You wouldn't believe how protective they were of me, both my parents. They worried all the time when I wasn't around.'

'You're very lucky,' James heard himself say, to his surprise. 'My parents were largely noticeable by their absence. Perhaps not with Izzy. She got the best of them because she was so much younger, but certainly Max had no real idea who they were, and neither, to a large extent, did I.'

He shot her a crooked smile, slightly embarrassed at that confession, and even more astonished that he rather liked that she had been the recipient. 'When you have all the money in the world, and the freedom to do whatever you want with it, without any parental control or discipline or interest, you'd be surprised how pointless it all seems.' He paused. 'Your mother has never met me. What she knows about me is what she's read in those lurid gossip articles…'

'I know. Again, I'm very sorry this isn't going to be as straightforward as you'd probably predicted.'

He waved down her apology. 'Stop telling me how sorry you are. You shouldn't be. If you're afraid that your mother will be disillusioned when she finds out what happened, then don't you think it's important that she meets me?'

'Meets you?' Ellie's mouth dropped open. Meet James Stowe? She tried to picture her anxious, diminutive mother, thrust into the presence of this over-the-top dynamic guy with the sharp, restless brain and the ridiculous good looks, and she visibly shuddered. 'Why would that help anything?'

'Think about it,' James murmured, one hundred percent of his attention focused on her. 'If you tell her that it was all a complete fabrication, then chances are she's not going to believe you. Even if she pretends to. You know what they say about no smoke without fire. Then she'll wonder why you might be lying and, whatever conclusion she reaches, she'll be disappointed.'

'Yes, well…' Ellie looked at him, a little flustered, because she had no great urge to give him a minute-by-minute rendition of what she intended to say to her mother, largely because the conversation was still a work in progress in her head.

'If you tell her the truth…that you and I were lovers…then from what she will have read in the gutter press, from what Naomi has managed to convey, she will assume that you were taken advantage of by me. How do you think she will feel about that?'

He didn't give her time to formulate an opinion on what he had just said, but seamlessly moved on. 'She'll either be heartbroken that her baby girl has let herself be seduced by a big, bad wolf, or else she'll be worried that your taste in men might be heading in the wrong direction. Or both.'

'I hadn't actually got as far as considering what…'

'You don't want any unintentional stress being put on her shoulders, do you?'

'Of course not!' The wretched man had a point, and it wasn't one she had considered. Her mother worried. Would she end up more worried after a frazzled explanation about what had actually happened? Disappointment that there would be no wedding bells after all was one thing. The fear that she, Ellie, might somehow have decided to abandon the moral code she had always lived by would be something altogether more difficult for her to deal with. Wouldn't it?

'Then here's what I suggest.'

His voice was softly bewitching, lulling and mesmerising her. He'd finished his glass of wine and she realised she had too. She'd barely been aware of drinking it! Part of her knew that she should deal with her mother on her own, that any suggestion that her boss climb into the picture would just be an added layer of complication she could do without, and yet…

She was seduced by his voice, by the certainty he conveyed that somehow everything was going to be all right…that if he came along the business with her mother would be sorted to a far more satisfactory degree. It was in his nature to take charge and he was good at it, and right now she *wanted* someone to take charge. She had been going out of her mind ever since her private life had been splattered across the tabloids.

'What's that?' She opened the door to whatever he was about to suggest.

'We both go to see your mother. We can fill her in on what happened, and at least she'll have a chance to see that I'm not the guy portrayed in those articles—the guy who messes around with women for his own enjoyment and was happy to do the same with you. We had a relationship, but it was consensual and enjoyable, and was our mutual choice to bring it to a close. Meeting me will take the drama out of the situation. And, when we've explained that to her, then we can see about filling in the rest of the world…'

CHAPTER EIGHT

WAITING BY THE window, peering out into the still grey light of a dull, rainy morning that hadn't quite broken, because it wasn't yet six, Ellie wondered how she had managed to be coaxed into this so easily.

But he had come through that front door behind which she had been hiding, he had taken control and she had been grateful.

She was also guiltily aware of feeling a sense of relief that someone else would be there when she broke the news to her mother that she wouldn't, after all, be walking down the aisle, followed swiftly by a trip to the hospital to give birth to those long-awaited grandchildren.

Ellie had known that her mum wanted her to settle down. It was almost as if she didn't think her job as a mother had been done well unless Ellie got married, had kids and lived happily ever after. Or at least, it would seem, *had a bit of fun*. Maybe that was part of the reason why she had been happy to see her go to Barbados. Maybe, when Ellie had had her back turned, worrying about her mother had changed into her mother worrying about *her*.

How was she to know that having fun would come at painful cost?

Did it make sense that James come with her? Overnight, she'd managed to justify it to herself. Yes, even though her mother would find out that any hat buying expeditions would have to be put on ice, at least she would see that the love affair had been a lovely time out, with neither one taking advantage of the other. She would see that there had been nothing sordid about it.

She wouldn't see the pain because Ellie would keep that to herself. She would be relieved that her daughter was finding her feet and stretching her wings, getting ready to fly.

A mature, adult fling. She felt giddy when she thought about her mother finding out that her baby was capable of a meaningless fling, even if it was with a guy she might actually approve of—because when James laid on the charm he was as close to irresistible as any human being could get.

James showed up on time, his sleek, black low-slung Porsche pulling up outside her house just as daylight was tentatively beginning to make an appearance. She watched for a few spellbound seconds as he vaulted smoothly out of the car, dressed entirely in black, and bounded up to her front door, which she pulled open before he could ring the doorbell.

'You're ready,' he said appreciatively. 'I wondered whether I'd get here to find you'd bolted your front door because you had a change of mind.' He bent to sweep up the small overnight bag she had packed and looked at her quizzically. 'Is this it?'

'I keep clothes at Mum's. I'm just taking a few essentials.' They'd agreed that he would come for one night because the trip was too long to go there and back in a day. She would stay on for a week or more while he returned to work and doused the flames of curiosity that would be blazing on the office floor. By the time she was ready to return, he had assured her with breezy confidence, everything would be entirely back to normal.

She believed him. It was one more nightmare he'd promised to sort out and she was willing to put her faith in that promise. Having always considered herself to be built of very stern stuff, given all the responsibilities she had taken on her shoulders from such a young age, she was amazed at just how pliable she was when it came to leaning on someone else.

'No nuisance calls overnight? No lurking men with cameras on the pavement this morning?'

They were walking towards his car and she slipped into the low, leather seat as he opened the boot of the car and slung in her bag.

'Nothing.' She felt a familiar tingle as he slid into the driver seat and briefly turned to look at her, one hand resting on the steering wheel, the other on his thigh.

In the barely there half-light his eyes glittered, boring straight into her. Since he'd descended on her, taking her by surprise, he had made no move whatsoever to touch her. In no way at all had he shown any interest in picking up where they had abruptly left off.

Yes, he had mentioned their relationship in passing, almost as an afterthought, and *of course* Ellie told herself that she was profoundly grateful for that closure.

The last thing she wanted was for him to put her in an impossible situation. No way under the sun would she welcome those sexy dark blue eyes on her, assessing, speculating, *encouraging* thoughts she knew were too close to the surface for her own good.

He had no idea what she felt, what was going on in her head, and she meant to keep it that way. He had no idea that his very lack of interest would be her source of strength when it came to recovering from her own foolish love.

And then, just as soon as her feet were back under the desk, she would start casually casting around for another job. She would explain, when the time came, that Barbados had opened her eyes to the possibility of a job where going abroad would feature more. She'd think of something to say, because she couldn't see a way of working alongside him indefinitely. Not feeling the way she did.

He switched on the engine and was manoeuvring along the narrow road, having programmed her mother's address into his satnav.

Now, she slanted disobedient eyes to the hand resting lightly on the gear stick and shivered. She despised the way she still wanted those hands to touch her, wanted those supple fingers to trail a burning path along her skin, to slip into the cleft between her legs, into her.

With the searing force of a branding iron, images of him were scored into her head, lodged so impossibly tightly that the tipping point between containment and despair, when she was with him now, felt as flimsy as a whisker.

'Good,' James returned with a note of smug satisfaction. 'I made a couple of calls. When you're in the public arena, it always pays to be cosy with a couple of the more senior of the paparazzi. There's a hierarchy there, and if you know how to use it it can come in useful. I let the word go out that they can have their story in a couple of days' time. Pursue, and they'll find connections they never knew they needed slamming the door on them.'

'Really?' Ellie was impressed.

'Really.' He half smiled. 'Most people know that getting on the wrong side of me isn't always the best way forward.'

'Well, thank you. It certainly helped with my sleeping last night.' She paused, and then continued in an awkward rush, 'I just want to thank you for making things easier for me. All of this…it's neither your fault nor mine. It's just something unexpected that happened, but you really have made dealing with the consequences…um…easier. You know—letting me have a week off work while you deal with the fallout there.'

'You're not accustomed to asking for help, are you?' he enquired softly and Ellie blushed, not looking at him, but staring straight ahead as he threaded through the narrow streets towards the motorway.

That was the sort of personal question he would never have asked her before they'd become involved, and it was just another reason why she knew she would have to quit her job just as soon as she could.

From passionate lover, he was now making his way to that awful place known as good friend… except he wasn't, was he? She didn't want him to adopt the role of being a shoulder she could cry on simply because he'd managed to get under her skin, just because they'd slept together, but she knew he would. He already was!

That would be the added dimension he had referred to, the one that would exist between them once their affair had run its course.

She projected to a point in the future when she would have to watch him hop back into the dating scene, returning to his normal luxury diet of catwalk models, as far as he was concerned, knowing she had returned to her quiet spot in the corner of the office—dutiful, efficient and once again background.

'Are you?' She threw the question back at him and he burst out laughing.

'Touché,' he said drily. 'Although, in fairness, why would I ever ask for help when I can handle pretty much everything myself?'

'You're so arrogant,' Ellie heard herself say, and then could have kicked herself for falling into the same trap he had…for going back to that place where they were intimate and where intimate things could be said without raising an eyebrow.

'So you've told me before. You wouldn't want me any other way.'

Ellie fidgeted, suddenly uncomfortable in the tight confines of his sports car.

Casting about for something inoffensive to say, he was the first to break the silence. 'So, tell me about your mother.'

'My mother?'

'What should I expect?'

'Does it matter? I mean, we're going there so that we can tell her face to face that this is all a storm in a teacup. I don't think you need to know what she's like, do you?'

'What's the point of my presence in that case? You want to smooth over anxieties your mother might have about this whole messy situation? Then I suggest you tell me about her so that I can emerge a sympathetic character as opposed to a serial womaniser who's used you for his own nefarious purposes and can barely show an interest in your only living relative. In which case, she might question my presence in her house in the first place.'

James could feel her tension. She was wired. Poor sleep, nervous tension. A strong person suddenly catapulted into uncertain, stormy seas without a lifebelt. It was pleasing to think that he was able to throw her that vital lifebelt. Having never seen himself in the role of knight in shining armour, primed to save damsels in distress, he was quietly pleased with himself now.

So much so that it overrode what he knew he should be feeling, namely intense rage that Naomi had dumped him from a very great height into the one situation she knew he would deeply resent. For the inveterate bachelor, widespread and incorrect rumours about getting married constituted a nightmare. On a personal level, it was a huge nuisance, and when the woman in question was someone like Ellie then it took on a whole new dimension.

Of course, Naomi was shrewd enough to have clocked that immediately. He would see that he returned the favour in due course, but for the moment he couldn't say that he was unhappy to find himself at the wheel of his Porsche, driving to Devon in the early hours of a grey autumn morning with his PA next to him. Nor did he harbour any regret about doing what he was doing for the sake of her mother, a woman he had never met and didn't know from Adam. He knew that her mother was mentally fragile and to help remove that one worry from her shoulders was the least he could do.

He slid a sideways glance at the small figure hunched in the deep leather seat, face averted as she stared through the window at nothing in particular. She was chewing her lower lip and he didn't have to see her face to know exactly what expression she would be wearing—the one of someone suddenly carrying the weight of the world on her shoulders.

A wave of protectiveness washed over him and he determined that when she returned to work it would be to find all her colleagues suitably silent on the matter of their publicised affair. Anyone who dared make her life uncomfortable would face his wrath. It was the least he could do.

He could handle a situation like this. Rumour…gossip…malice. He could handle them because he had become emotionally untouchable. But for the first time that was something that failed to soothe. Was it that laudable to make a habit of avoiding anything that smacked of involvement? It was a question that had never bothered him before but for some reason it bothered him now. He brushed his unease aside.

'So you were telling me about your mother…?'

Ellie sighed and gave up. What was the point in being tight-lipped on the subject anyway?

When she looked back at herself as she'd used to be—working for him, aloof, professional, utterly private—it was like looking at a stranger from a distance. He had managed to invade every nook and cranny of her life and this trip to Devon would be the final battering down of everything she had kept so closely guarded, whether through habit or design.

'My mum's not old. In her mid-sixties. My parents had me when they were quite old, which is probably why they were always so protective. They'd tried and had just about given up when I came along. When I think about it, they were a unit for such a long time, just the pair of them, that they were both very dependent on one another. And my mum's always been quite gentle, with Dad the one taking the lead.'

'So when he died…'

'It was so unexpected. Barely any time to adjust. Yes, when my dad died, my mum's frailty really came to the fore. Since then, she's found a niche where she lives. She has her book club, and she gardens and bakes cakes for the local Women's Institute. But what worries me is that it's almost as if she's been waiting all this time for something like this to happen—for me to find a guy and get married and settle down. I mean, I *knew* she hankered after grandchildren. She always makes a point of faithfully reporting each and every friend whose son or daughter had a baby…'

James burst out laughing. 'Not very subtle, in other words!'

Ellie grinned, relaxed a little, looked at him and felt that swoop of bursting love and affection inside her, however unwelcome the sensation might be.

'Not very. The point is that I would have told her immediately that this was all a load of nonsense, would have explained the situation on the phone, but I didn't want to take any chances with her getting stressed out and worried.'

'Maybe she's not quite as delicate as you think.'

'You could be right,' Ellie mused, a little startled at that shrewd observation, which was one she had slowly begun to reach for herself. Yet she wasn't certain enough of her mother's strength to take chances. 'Who knows? You might change your mind when you meet her.'

And, James thought, *I am meeting her...*

And he realised that he was looking forward to the prospect…

The skies were grey when the sleek sports car finally began the winding conclusion of the trip from London. They had driven through a series of towns and hamlets of varying sizes, passing silent churches and small open markets that were beginning to bustle into life as the day took shape.

Finally James pulled up in front of a small cottage that formed part of a cluster, all nestled with their own perfectly groomed gardens, tucked away in the maze of lanes and tiny tree-lined streets skittering in the foothills of the mighty Exmoor.

They had driven through a small village just big enough to house essentials for a small community, dominated by a picturesque church that sat squarely in a rectangle of perfectly manicured lawns, its doors wide open to welcome whoever wanted to enter.

This couldn't have been more out of James's comfort zone. A life of privilege and access to everything money could buy had never provided him with any insight into the life of someone living in a tiny rural community.

He took a few seconds to look at the house in front of him. It was small and cream with a path to the front door that resembled something a child might have drawn, winding and cobbled and bordered by a bank on either side of neat grass, which was in turn fringed by equally neat hedges.

James breathed in deeply and shot a look at the girl next to him as she hesitated briefly. On the spur of the moment, he grasped her hand and, somewhere inside him, was gratified when she didn't let it go.

Ellie felt the warmth of his fingers curling

into hers and didn't think twice about curling her fingers right back into his, even after they left the car.

But she dropped her hand the second her mother opened the front door before the knocker had had time stop reverberating through the cottage.

'Mum!'

'Ellie! Darling!'

Angela Thompson was a small, thin woman with a face that would have been quite striking had it been plumper and less careworn. Her eyes were large and dark, her hair just touching her shoulders, as straight as her daughter's but threaded with grey. She had the look of someone who had spent far too much time crying.

Just at the moment she was beaming, however, and for the very first time Ellie remembered the carefree woman her mother used to be. The hug she received was warm and long, then her mother stepped back and eyed James, assessing him.

'Very nice,' she said approvingly.

Ellie's mouth fell open. 'Mum, this is…er…'

'I know. I've read all about you.' She stepped back to allow them both to brush past her, and *en passant* James inclined his head to kiss her on each cheek, French-style.

The cottage smelled of fresh bread and everywhere was sparkling. Cleaned in honour of the prospective son-in-law, Ellie thought with dismay… And *fresh bread*? Once upon a million years ago her mother had loved baking, but that had all been put on hold for so many years that it was a struggle to remember just when her mum had last baked anything at all.

With increasing alarm, she pondered this development while absently recognising that somehow James had managed to take control of the conversation, chatting about the drive down, answering questions about Barbados, all this as they were guided into the airy kitchen where ingredients were arranged for a hearty breakfast.

'You must be exhausted after your long drive…maybe you'd like to head up to your bedroom for a quick freshen-up?'

'Bedroom?' Ellie parroted weakly, surfacing slowly to the fact that dismantling her mother's misconception was going to be a more uphill task than she had first thought. Yes, her mother had sounded pleased and happy down the disembodied cell phone, but now, here in the flesh, Ellie was shocked at just how *alive* Angela Thompson was, just how *animated*.

'Of course. I've made up the guest room for the both of you.' She smiled and *winked*. 'Darling, your room just has that silly single bed, which wouldn't do at all. Now, why don't you both take your bags up? In the meantime, I'll start breakfast. Bacon fine for the pair of you? Eggs? I've got the most wonderful free-range eggs from Joan's chickens.'

'This is *awful*,' was the first thing Ellie said just as soon as the bedroom door was shut. She stared at James and tried to ignore the double bed dominating the small room and the vase of freshly picked flowers on the old-fashioned dressing table with the triple mirror. 'Are you *listening*?' she hissed, as he calmly peered through the window to the back garden and the acres of open countryside beyond.

'I'm listening.'

Ellie advanced a couple of steps into the bedroom. She'd dumped her small holdall on the bed and only now noticed that he had deposited his black leather overnight bag next to hers. They sat there, touching, like a couple of mocking reminders of the time they had spent in bed together.

Annoyed, she snatched hers and dumped it on the chair by the dressing table.

'What are we going to do?'

'I'm confused by your use of the plural. Haven't I already done my bit?'

'You've done more than just *your bit*.' Ellie thought of her mother preening and gazing at him, clearly mentally uploading photos of him as her future son-in-law about whom she would be able to boast to all the neighbours.

'Explain.'

'You…you… There was no need to go overboard with the charm!' Ellie exclaimed despairingly.

'I thought we'd agreed that it would be a good idea for me not to be cast in the role of ruthless, womanising cad? I thought…'

He paused and looked at her with his head tilted to one side. 'I thought we'd come to the conclusion that if you didn't want your mother unduly worrying it would be a good idea for her to at least understand that what we shared did not involve you being taken advantage of. Or, worse, didn't involve you losing all sense of good judgement—at which point she might imagine that you were setting a precedent for making up for lost time by having random sex with guys who were no good for you?'

'Yes, but…'

'But nothing, Ellie. I'm here because you've been thrown into the deep end by Naomi and, believe it or not, I accept a great deal of responsibility for that. I'm willing to do what I can to level the playing field, but don't forget that my presence here is for your benefit.' He shrugged. 'Left to me, I would brush off the inconvenient rumours without thinking too hard about it.'

'I know.' Ellie sighed. Could she blame him for being himself? He charmed. Could she blame her mother for warming to his charm? No.

She'd always had the choice to do what he would have done—to shrug off the inconvenient rumours without going into a tailspin. She could have explained everything to her mother over the telephone. She could have braved out the curiosity and gossip at work, knowing that everything faded in the fullness of time.

She hadn't, so here she was, and she surely couldn't start laying into him for just playing the part she'd asked him to play?

Which didn't mean that she didn't despair of the situation.

'I'll sort it out,' she assured him. 'You stay put here. Unpack. Have a shower. No *en suite* bathroom, but there's one at the end of the landing. Mum's probably put towels in there for us.' She tried to conceal a treacherous shiver at the thought of him standing naked under the shower, face upturned, eyes closed as the water poured over his impressive body. 'I don't care what you do but let me have half an hour or so to fill her in. The scenery outside is amazing. You can… er…stare through the window and appreciate it.'

Ellie didn't give him time to muse on the joys of doing what she'd just told him to do. She raced down to the kitchen to find her mother busily setting the pine table. In the centre there was bunch of freshly picked flowers in a vase. The bread was out of the oven and Ellie's mouth watered.

Her mother was pottering, humming something under her breath, and for a just a second Ellie was catapulted back in time to when her dad had still been alive…when *this* was what life had been like…when life for her mother had been a place where humming took place and baking was a thing of pleasure.

She breathed in deeply and stepped forward with a smile pinned to her face.

James gave her half an hour. Picturesque though the scenery was, indeed as beautiful in its own grey majesty as the blistering blue skies on the opposite side of the world, there was only so much he could stare at when his mind was busy trying to project to whatever scene was taking place in the kitchen downstairs.

He couldn't even focus on his laptop, which said something. For the first time, he felt as though he had walked, eyes wide open, into a situation the likes of which he had never dealt with before. He didn't do personal dramas when it came to women. He had never allowed himself to fall victim to the one thing he loathed, namely the idiocy of getting so wrapped up with a woman that you ended up straying into her dilemmas, having views on problems that had nothing to do with him…

He was discomforted by the realisation that this wasn't his comfort zone, and he could only placate his feverish brain by reminding himself that this was a temporary break in proceedings and that normal life would resume in no time at all.

In fact, he mused, pulling open the bedroom door and resisting the urge to take the stairs two at a time, he wouldn't be here at all were it not for Naomi and her mischief-making. He would be in Hawaii, soaking up more sun, doing the whole work, women and song thing and catching up with his brother pre-wedding. He would be relishing some healthy distraction! He enjoyed women. Women enjoyed him. But, when he thought about enjoying the joys of *anything* with another woman, his mind went blank and he felt as though he was staring into a fog.

He heard Angela's voice through the kitchen door which was ajar, and he paused, not so much trying to hear what was being said as wondering how he should approach this situation, given Ellie would have broken the disappointing news to her mother that they were not the couple she had been led to believe. He barely recognised the alien sensation that momentarily swept through him as indecision, so accustomed was he to having complete control of whatever situation he happened to find himself in…

He pushed aside the unfamiliar feeling and nudged open the door. The first thing he saw was Ellie smiling, smiling and smiling, as though her face might crack at any second.

And, in that instant, he knew exactly what was going on.

How much deeper could this hole get? Ellie thought, wrung out at the end of a day that seemed to have stretched to infinity and beyond.

Aside from escaping briefly just before their early six o'clock dinner, so that she could finally get to the shower and have some tormented down-time to herself, she had been on the go. Fending off questions, feeling the incisive boring of James's eyes on her, wherever she went, trying hard not to stare down at the calamitous abyss opening up at her feet. And, of course, silently thanking her boss for not cornering her so that he could ask the one question that must surely be on the tip of his tongue…

What the hell is going on?

She owed him an explanation but she was dreading what she foresaw as a showdown. He'd done her a favour in returning to London to rescue her from her own inexperience in dealing with the nightmare that had landed in her lap. He owed her. That would have been his take on things. Even if they hadn't slept together, he would have seen her as *his* responsibility in any kind of awkward situation that might have been generated by him, because, put simply, he was one of the good guys, however tough and uncompromising he might be in the work arena.

Her mother retired early, at a little after eight, to read and have a bath and absorb the day's events.

Kitchen clean and counters wiped, Ellie finally allowed herself to be cornered. Rather, barricaded in, because James positioned himself at the door of the kitchen, arms folded, eyebrows raised, and looked at her for a few seconds in silence.

Like her, he had escaped to have a shower earlier on, after their hearty breakfast at almost midday and tea in the garden at four. He was in a pair of faded jeans, a grey long-sleeved tee shirt that lovingly and unfairly emphasised his lean muscularity and some tan loafers that would have cost the earth.

'So...' he drawled. 'Help me out here, Ellie. I thought, after I'd spent half an hour staring out at the great British scenery, that I would come down to the kitchen to find your mother semi-tearful but resigned, in front of a cup of tea, having received the disappointing news that there wasn't going to be any happy-ever-after…'

'I know.' Ellie shot him a guilty look from under her lashes. She indicated one of the chairs by the table, thought better of it and then moved to the back door that led out into the garden. She needed some fresh air, even if the air was a little too fresh for what she was wearing. Leading the way, she unhooked her old mac from the door and stepped into a pair of wellies, even though it wasn't raining.

Her mother's garden was small and manageable but gave the illusion of being absolutely enormous because it backed onto open fields. With just the light from the kitchen behind them, the garden was shrouded in darkness, and beyond the fields rose and fell with dark uniformity, much like the ocean at night, the very ocean they had left behind.

Ellie didn't look at him as she straightened one of the garden chairs and curled up into it, tucking her legs under her, covering them with the mac. She felt the brush of his arm against hers as he adopted a similar position, both of them staring out at the vast landscape.

Her skin tingled from that accidental brush, making her shiver with that unwelcome sexual awareness that had dogged her all day.

He'd been the perfect gentleman. He'd charmed

her mother and had been unfailingly considerate towards her, and Ellie had hated every second of it, because it wasn't what she wanted from him. *Not any more.* She wanted passion and fire and craving, and all that hunger that had flared in his eyes every time he'd looked at her a million years ago in Barbados…

The wretched hopelessness of it engulfed her. She could no longer summon up any enthusiasm for the prospect of slowly weaning herself off him. All she could see was a guy who didn't love her and anguished days spent working alongside him, watching him carry on with his life while she was cruelly rooted in the past, desperately trying to move on but condemned to become a spectator to other women taking her place in his bed.

'I couldn't do it,' she said sadly. 'I really tried, but I just couldn't bring myself to do it…'

CHAPTER NINE

'I REALISE YOU'RE probably quite annoyed...' *Livid*, she mentally amended. 'I prepared my speech. I was going to be light-hearted about it, tell Mum that it was all just a silly mistake... that that's what happens when a vindictive ex is in the picture...'

She sighed.

'But then she rushed into telling me about how happy she was...overjoyed... How long she'd spent worrying that life was passing me by... I was hell-bent on taking care of her, and didn't see that somewhere along the line she really just wanted me to take care of myself. Now she thinks that I'm finally happy, that I've found the one for me.'

'I understand,' James murmured.

'She started crying, but in a quiet way. Said how lost she'd felt after Dad died, that she'd been a burden to me and that it was so wonderful to finally see me happy, and actually living life the way it should be lived. I think those were her exact words.'

What Ellie failed to mention were the other things Angela Thompson had said. She had spotted them holding hands through the window, before she'd answered the door. She could see how much love there was between them. She'd been feeling so low, but now she felt as though she'd been given a new lease of life…

Every smiling confidence had plunged the dagger deeper into Ellie's heart. No longer could glib explanations gloss over what had happened, yet how on earth could she go into the detail of how she *really* felt about her emotionally unavailable boss? How could she make sense for her mother of the way she had meandered, eyes wide open, into an emotional quagmire, where she was now stuck loving him while he turned his back and walked away? How could she tell her mum that what had started between them had only started because she had just been so different from his glamorous ex? From *all* his glamorous exes? That she had been the new and different toy with which he had enjoyed playing for a while but was never going to hold on to for very long?

Every joyous utterance from her mother had been a cruel reminder of just how far from the truth she was. In the end, Ellie had cravenly backed away from the confession she had been intent on making.

'I… She knows you won't be staying beyond tomorrow. I told her you had urgent business to see to in London. You'll be leaving first thing.'

'You're upset,' James murmured, eyes shielded.

'Of course I'm upset!' Ellie burst out in angry frustration. She strode towards the bed and flung herself on it, utterly exhausted and angry with him for being so calm. But then what was at stake for him, really? After this interlude, life would return to normal quickly. She would be the one left picking up pieces. She would be the one having to deal with her mother's bitter disappointment after he'd swanned off, having done his bit. And that didn't even begin to cover the horror of dealing with her broken heart.

She rested her arm over her eyes, banking down a desire to cry. She knew he had joined her on the bed when his weight depressed the mattress. She tensed, wanting him so badly that it hurt, yet refusing to yield to the fierce physical pull he had over her. She kept her arm draped over her face.

She didn't expect him to scoop her up, but he did, and she didn't struggle when he enfolded her in his arms and rested her head against his shoulder.

A kind and caring gesture, she thought as her body began to stir into heated response.

He stroked her back and she was dimly aware of him murmuring soothing things under his breath. She began to relax. She didn't want to make love. She *knew* that that was a place she no longer had a right to revisit. Yet they did, slowly and tenderly, and it felt as though everything was happening in a dream. He held her for a long time, coaxing her anxieties out of her, stroking her hair until she was melting against him, eyes closed, her breathing evening out.

Thoughts flew out of her head as fast as her anxieties. Her mind went a complete blank and familiar sensations settled in to replace the arousal of her body, her breasts becoming tender, her nipples pinching and then hardening into tight buds as his hand slipped under her top to caress her. He knew her body so well, could strum it with the dexterity of a maestro.

She didn't open her eyes. She allowed herself to be seduced into trance-like pleasure, opening up to him with the hunger of someone deprived of sustenance for too long.

Her clothes were removed. She felt the coolness of the night on her naked skin and his silent, caressing fingers on her, touching her in places she had come to love being touched and sending her body up in flames.

Neither of them spoke and it felt as if they were both in the same place, contemplative and aware that there would be a situation to deal with when this brief interlude was over. But, for the moment, Ellie *needed* this, whether it made sense or not.

He nuzzled her breasts and explored her body, gently caressing her between her legs and feeling the wetness of her arousal, and she did the same for him, pleasuring him with her hands and her mouth until he was groaning, low, husky and urgent. They were moving in slow motion, languorous and fluid. He went between her legs, tasting her with his mouth and his tongue, flicking and teasing her clitoris while she coiled her fingers into his hair, clinging like someone needing anchorage in a storm.

He didn't stop. He wanted her to come against his questing mouth and she wanted it as well. It felt right. She moved against him, squirming, her breathing fast and shallow, and then she came in a spasm, arching up while he continued to probe her most intimate place with his tongue. His hand rested on her belly, tugging so that the sensations were so powerful that she had to stifle the urge to cry out loud with pleasure.

She breathed him in as he rose up to straddle her, and opened her eyes only once to see him take his manhood in his hand, circling it firmly but gently, pleasuring himself while she cupped him in her hands and rose to delicately lick the veined hardness.

He came on her, a hot splash that she rose to greet with her mouth, savouring its saltiness while the sadness she had kept at bay began permeating back into her.

Exhausted, she could barely utter a word when, after what felt like dreamy hours, he lay next to her. She curled against him, fighting sleep but unable to resist it, and the next time she opened her eyes a thin, grey light was seeping through the curtains into the bedroom.

She struggled into a sitting position, disoriented for a few seconds, then registering what had happened the night before.

Also registering that the space next to her was empty and, glancing at her phone at the side of the bed, that it was a little after six in the morning.

Early.

While the thoughts were still foggy in her head, the bedroom door opened and in he walked, as stealthy as a big cat, not bothering to turn on the light, instead making for the bed and perching on the side. Aside from a towel wrapped round his lower half, he was naked, and she closed her eyes and breathed in deeply as she tried to get her thoughts into some kind of order.

'How long have you been awake?' she asked, heart thundering inside her, reacting all over again to the intense pull of his masculinity.

'Not long. Long enough to have a shower and do some thinking.'

He looked at her, pink and sleepy-eyed, her hair tousled, just the slope of her narrow shoulders visible because she had pulled the duvet up to her chin, which she rested on her knees. There were instances, thoughts that flashed through his head, that made it impossible to remember her as his dutiful PA.

None of this had gone according to plan. He had anticipated something clear cut, possibly a bit uncomfortable but largely sanitised. He had anticipated a situation he would walk away from, dusting his hands free of complications that he had told himself he could do without. They had slept together but there had been a finite time limit imposed on what they'd had, and at no point had it really occurred to him that that time limit might end up going off-piste so accustomed was he to exercising complete control over all aspects of his life.

He'd done the right thing in returning to London once the story had hit the press and he had done the right thing in suggesting they faced her mother. He had accepted responsibility for the fact that none of this would have happened had he not dumped his ex and then turned his attentions to the one woman he should never have contemplated going anywhere near, whatever her hidden attractions.

Had he planned to sleep with her again?

He honestly didn't know.

Common sense had prevailed once, but he was honest enough to acknowledge that it had flown out of the window the minute he had returned from Barbados to find her holed up in her house, like a prisoner terrified of a firing squad positioned outside the front door. Every protective instinct he'd never known he had had kicked in with stupendous force.

Was that what had reawakened the attraction he had been confident of putting to bed? Had the novelty of new sensations propelled him into wanting to light that fire all over again?

Yet he had managed to hang on to his common sense, had managed to look at the bigger picture and take on board the role he knew he had to play to assuage her mother's fears and doubts.

He had chatted to her mother but, all the while, his eyes had strayed to Ellie, who'd been as nervous as a kitten. He had noted her interaction with her mother, had seen the concern and love there. He intuited the pain she would feel at the thought of crushing her mother's optimistic, romantic dreams. He knew what pain felt like, how it could sear a hole right through you until you were dazed with it, and something inside him had twisted.

Guilt? A conscience?

Was that why he had been driven to sleep with her again? Because his conscience had been pricked? Because he had seen her tremulous fear of letting her mother down and had recognised, guiltily, that he had put her in that position?

Or was it just a case of something started that had ended prematurely?

James did not underestimate the power of sexual attraction. He'd still wanted her, whatever label he chose to put on it, and she still wanted him. Their relationship had not behaved according to the rules he had laid down, but weren't there always exceptions to rules?

He had been adamant that things would need to stop so that normal working relations between them could resume after he returned from Max's wedding. He'd always kept his working life very separate from his love life. However, the two had merged, and maybe this was just something they both needed to finish. It wasn't about emotions, it was about finishing a chapter that had been started. They were both adults and she had her head screwed on. Why should it interfere with the excellent working relationship they both had?

Her grey eyes, locked on him, were wary. He raked his fingers through his hair and noted the way she swallowed, all too aware of him just as he was all too aware of her.

'Last night…' he murmured.

'I know. Shouldn't have happened.' Ellie looked at him defensively.

'But it did,' he said gently.

'I was in a poor place. Things hadn't worked out the way I thought they would…' She glared at him accusingly. Why couldn't he just leave it be? she wondered fiercely. Why did he have to drag everything out in the open for an early-morning post-mortem?

The way she had succumbed to him, given herself to him, was a cruel reminder of just how much she loved him and how much she had so foolishly invested in him.

'No,' he agreed. 'And, trust me, I can understand your dilemma.' She failed to fill in the gaps so he continued, his voice soothing and sinfully seductive. 'Your mother is fully invested in this business about us being an item. She's spent the past few years despairing of you ever meeting someone.'

'That's a massive overstatement!'

'And now here we are. She likes me…'

'There was no need to go overboard with the James Stowe charm.'

'I had no idea that that was what I was doing.'

'I had hoped that she might see us together and realise how ill-suited we were to one another, but you had to lay it on thick.'

'You can't blame me for being myself—'

'I tried to point out the glaring differences between us,' Ellie interjected bitterly, thinking of her valiant, doomed attempts to get things back on track. 'I told her the sort of background you came from, the life you were accustomed to leading. I reminded her that, once reality kicks in, things begin to fade…'

'And she wasn't buying any of it?'

Ellie shook her head curtly. She decided not to mention her mother's response to all those genuine and true observations. She had listened, her head tilted to one side, a smile tugging at her lips, and philosophically had told her that she recognised what love looked like.

Besides, she had added, hitting below the belt with the unerring accuracy only a devoted parent could bring to the table, 'I know you and I know you would never hop into bed with a man just for the sake of it. You're just not that type of girl and you never have been.'

'Maybe she needs to see first-hand that things don't always go according to plan,' he said thoughtfully, and Ellie frowned.

'What are you talking about?'

'Last night happened for a reason,' he ruminated. 'And that reason had nothing to do with the fact that you were in need of comfort…'

Ellie reddened. Outside the sounds of the day beginning infiltrated the bedroom, the early-morning greyness gradually turning into weak sunshine and trying its best to get past the curtains.

'You still want me,' he forced out into the open, just what she didn't want to acknowledge, and she closed her eyes for a few seconds, her breathing quickening while she desperately wished that she was somewhere else. 'It's nothing to be ashamed of,' he murmured, trailing his finger along her jaw with such devastating effect that her breath hitched in her throat and her eyes fluttered open.

'It's mutual. I still want you. I never saw this coming,' he admitted with roughened honesty. 'I never thought any of this would happen, but it did. When we were in Barbados, I saw this as unexpected but temporary. Fun for a few days until fate decided otherwise. I still want you, so why not continue what we have? You can't bring yourself to tell your mother that this isn't going to end up in marriage, and she can't see it because we only ever see what we want to see, and what your mother wants to see is you with me.

'Maybe she needs to see us have this relationship and then, when it inevitably fizzles out, she'll accept that it was something that wasn't meant to be, with all the best intentions in the world. Maybe, that's what the hungry paparazzi needs to see… Instead of mounting a defence, maybe we just need to go with the flow and let what we have run its course…'

Ellie listened to all of this in stunned silence. She knew exactly where he was going with this. When it came to women, James liked to be the one who called the shots. He was always the one who ended things. Like a toddler with a never-ending supply of brand-new toys, he enjoyed the freedom to dispose of one toy exactly when he wanted before moving on to the next.

He was being perfectly honest when he told her that he hadn't foreseen things happening the way they had. Even when they *had* ended up in bed together, he had still not foreseen wanting to continue what had started against all the odds.

It would fizzle out. It was, in his words, *inevitable.* She wasn't one of his drop-dead gorgeous supermodels. She was his efficient, very ordinary-looking personal assistant. He had been charmed by the novelty, but he had always assumed that the novelty would wear thin very quickly. It hadn't and, because it hadn't, he now saw no reason why they shouldn't continue what they had until it did.

On every level, he was a sensualist.

Into the lengthening silence, he continued without hesitation, his self-assurance growing by the second. 'You're speechless,' he said with satisfaction. 'I get it. It's not a solution either of us ever thought of because we were both sold on the notion that everything had to be neatly wrapped up before start of play. We broke up because… I suppose I got a little spooked. I got the sense that you might have been reaching out for some kind of emotional involvement. We broke up, but it doesn't mean that what we had was *broken*. We wanted each other then and we still want each other.'

'Sorry?' Ellie felt as though she had suddenly been plunged into an alternate universe where perfectly understandable words and sentences were reaching her as unintelligible mutterings in a foreign language.

Yes, she knew where he was going with this, but she couldn't credit his massive misinterpretation of her expression and her silence. How could someone so smart and so perceptive be so dense?

'We both thought that a few days in Barbados would get this out of our system. We both knew that it was a flash-in-the-pan situation. Still is, but the fire under the pan is taking a little longer than we anticipated to die out…that's the power of lust.'

'I don't think you understand…' Ellie said slowly.

He raised his eyebrows and smiled with the smooth confidence of a guy who had never been wrong-footed by a woman before in his life. He smiled with the utter confidence of a guy in complete control of his life and the outcome of the decisions he made. Right now he had decided that he wanted to carry on with what they had, and on the surface Ellie knew that every aspect of what he was suggesting made sense.

To him.

Because he wasn't involved. Because the ending was inevitable. Because as far as he was concerned they were on the same page…just two adults who had had a bit of fun…so why not drift into having a bit more fun until the whole thing became boring and petered out? Sure, he'd been *spooked*, but he was willing to overlook that, was willing to write that off as a by-product of their mutual physical attraction.

And suddenly she realised that returning to work and pretending that nothing had happened while she hunted around for another job wasn't going to do. Nor would she be able to return to work while trying to masquerade as the perfect PA she'd used to be, keeping her emotions in check while she was in front of her computer and at her desk, simmering in anticipation until they could sneak out, at separate times, to reunite in a blaze of passion somewhere.

It all felt overwhelming and seedy, and she was terrified of being tempted into a situation that would end up destroying her.

How easy it would be to mentally shut the door behind which the inevitable would be waiting for her. How easy it had been to jump into bed with him in the first place and then to stay there, living in an unreal bubble which she had known all along was going to burst. How easy it had been to kid herself that everything would be fine because she couldn't possibly fall in love with someone like James Stowe.

'How long do you think it would last?' she asked, her voice curious and conversational 'You know…the sleeping together…until the inevitable happens?'

Taken aback, he was silent for a few seconds, frowning and then giving her question bemused house room.

'How long is a piece of string?' he said eventually, and shrugged. 'Does it matter? It's not something we can put a timeline on…'

'No, I don't suppose it would be,' Ellie intoned coolly.

'We tried the timeline before,' he dismissed

impatiently, 'and it didn't work. Why bother trying to pin things down this time round?'

'Why indeed?'

'What's going on here?' He looked at her, eyes narrowed, trying to get inside her head. She could see that, could sense it, could sense his growing bewilderment that the plan he had decided upon was not quite going in the direction he had anticipated.

'Us carrying on? It's not going to happen, James.'

'Your reason being…?' He smiled slowly, eyes darkening, and she fought to combat the swirl of hot sensation that slow smile so effortlessly unleashed inside her.

'You're right when you say that I didn't expect…what happened between us to happen.' Ellie inhaled deeply and stared down at a dizzying abyss yawning open beneath her.

'Neither of us did, believe me…'

'I have always been serious when it comes to guys and relationships. I said as much to you.' She smiled sadly. 'Which is probably why I have so little experience.'

'When did you ever have time for relationships? You were responsible from a young age for the well-being of your mother.'

Ellie ignored the genuine empathy in his voice because that was just what had got her into hot water in the first place. His easy ability to empathise…a personality that was tuned in to those around him in ways that were instinctive and seductive.

He didn't have women running around behind him, weeping and wailing when things crashed and burned, because he was rich and good-looking. His charms lay way beyond those narrow parameters and she had been short sighted not to have clocked that earlier on, when her heart had still been intact.

'I guess,' she said, 'I absorbed how close my parents were, and knew deep down that that was the sort of relationship I wanted for myself. I wasn't brought up to indulge in wild flings and one-night stands but, James, that's pretty much what happened, isn't it?'

'It was certainly wild, but a one-night stand it most definitely wasn't.'

'I thought I would be able to enjoy what we had, and walk away from it with only a bit of a dusting down necessary before everything returned to normal, but I was wrong.'

'What do you mean?'

There was a guarded edge to his voice that Ellie couldn't miss.

'I should have asked myself how it was that it turned out being so easy to just fall into bed with you.'

'Sometimes, when the atmosphere is just right…' A sudden wicked grin chased away the wariness that had been there before. 'Hot sun… white sand…blue sea… It's a recipe for sex between two consenting adults who're attracted to one another.'

'James, I never thought I could fall for a guy like you, but I did.'

Ellie watched as the lingering smile on his face disappeared. Comprehension followed swiftly. He was adding up and making sense of all those things that should have been a giveaway but which he had ignored, missed or misinterpreted.

'I don't get what you're trying to say.'

'You do, James,' Ellie told him gently.

She wondered whether he was thinking that this was a Naomi moment all over again. Another romp in the hay with someone he'd assumed was as casual as he was. She almost felt sorry for him.

'I could pretend,' she continued, watching as the colour drained from his face. 'That I don't feel the way I do. I know it would make life a lot easier for you but, when I walk away from this, I don't want to walk away with things left unsaid. I don't regret what happened between us, but I would regret *that*. I *would* regret thinking that I hadn't told you how I felt.'

Looking at her, James was aware of the cogs in his head working way below their usual optimum, whirring efficiency. His thoughts were blurry, even though he knew exactly what she was saying, just as he knew exactly how he should be reacting.

With horror. He hadn't signed up for this. He'd signed up for a few days of fun. Uppermost in his mind, however, was one overriding thought… *What's wrong with a bit of pretence? Whoever said that honesty was always the best policy needs to have a major rethink...*

'Of course,' he heard her continue calmly, 'I realise that this puts us in an untenable position, so I do have a suggestion.'

'You have a suggestion…'

How could they possibly be having this conversation here? In a bedroom? Barely dressed? Was that why he was finding it so difficult to focus? Why his thoughts were all over the place?

'My mum knows that you're due to leave today, that you could only pop down for an overnight stay because of work. You can get dressed and leave now, before she's up and moving about. She takes her time in the morning. I know you're probably going to think that I'm leaving you in the lurch workwise, but I won't, and you have my word on that.'

'Work hadn't yet crossed my mind.' James gritted his teeth.

Ellie ignored the barely audible interruption. 'I will remain here for a few days and this time, without you around, I can begin to lay the foundations for why things won't work out between us.'

'Fill me in, Ellie. I'm all ears.'

'First and foremost,' she said slowly, 'the hours you work. Too long. The very fact you had to dash off early in the morning because of business. I've worked for you, so I know how dedicated you are to your work, to the exclusion of everything else. Maybe I thought I could deal with that, but I was wrong. You go to Hawaii in a couple of days and, once you leave, I will return to the office and start sourcing my replacement.'

'You'll have to brace yourself for the wagging tongues...'

'I know,' Ellie told him quietly. 'But I will, because I intend to take responsibility for this, and not cower and hide away. When everything first blew up, I literally felt like a rabbit caught in the headlights, but that's not me.'

'No. It's not.'

'I've faced up to this situation, faced up to the fact that I made a terrible mistake in falling for you. But I guess...' she smiled wistfully '... that's something you're used to.'

She paused and aired the thought that had earlier crossed her mind. 'Poor Naomi was guilty of the same breach of the rules, but you don't have to worry that there will be any "kiss and tell" revelations. I intend to stay below the radar and, if anyone decides to camp out on the doorstep, then they'll be treated to such a diet of "no comment" that they'll give up in boredom.'

Accustomed as he was to taking complete charge of any situation involving women, James stared at her for a few silent seconds, digesting what she had just said.

She had spared him the discomfort of having to end things and he decided that he was grateful for that reprieve. Naturally, he would have had to sever all ties in the end, despite his initial suggestion that they let what they had play out until it had reached a natural conclusion. He didn't do emotional commitment and she had always known that.

Where she had lived with the calamitous effects of what happened when love didn't work out the way you expected it to, she had still clung to the romance of falling in love, to relationships that stayed the course, sailing towards happy-ever-after endings. Perhaps because, unlike his parents, hers had been devoted to her. For him, unheard and barely visible to both his parents, love equalled pain. So, while she still had faith in its existence, he had none. That was just the way it was.

She had read the situation perfectly. It was a relief, he determined. Now was his cue to take his leave, yet he remained pinned to the spot, frowning, then finally said, 'Forget about the replacement or coming into the office and facing down whatever gossip is sure to be circulating.'

He thought of her discomfort, of her putting on a brave face and battling through it, head down, betraying nothing of her inner turmoil. His brilliant PA would be back in place, calm and unflappable, though this time in the face of a nightmarish twist of fate.

She'd been right when she'd said that she had reacted emotionally to the sudden onslaught of paparazzi and their vulture-like curiosity. She would have done, he thought, because she wasn't battle-hardened as he was.

She was also head over heels in love with him and that wouldn't have helped matters...

He thought back to those amazing eyes lazy on him, intent veiled… He thought of the slow, low murmurs as she'd moved under his exploring hands…the feathery whisper of her fingers trailing along his body, touching him in a way that had never failed to set his body ablaze with an insane craving… It shook him.

'Take as long as you want when it comes to

letting your mother down gently.' He took the lead from her but his voice was unsteady as he killed wayward thoughts and focused on moving forward. Habits of a lifetime took over. When it came to women, moving forward was what he did.

'I can make a list of potential candidates to replace me,' Ellie said stiffly.

He was relieved that she was walking away. He couldn't wait to be rid of her now that she had told him how she felt.

Under her stony expression, her heart was breaking in two, but she would not regret the confession that had left her lips. It was called walking away with a clean slate. Unfortunately, the clean slate opened up the reality that she would have to find another job, and the chances of it being as well paid, not to mention satisfying, were slim.

'No need.' He began moving off, gathering belongings and chucking them into the hold-all he had brought with him.

'And don't worry about pay.' He glanced over his shoulder. 'I'll make sure you remain paid in full until you find another job, whenever that may be.'

They stared at one another in heated silence for a few electrifying seconds, and he was the first to spin round on his heels, his body rigid with furious tension.

She could barely watch as he got dressed, his back to her. What else was left to say when he was at the bedroom door, bag in hand, ready to go?

Nothing.

She lay down and rolled onto her side, turning away, waiting until she heard the soft click of the bedroom door being shut behind him.

CHAPTER TEN

No comment!

Sprawled in his expensive leather chair in front of his wood and steel desk, James glared at the computer screen winking at him, demanding a level of attention he was incapable of giving.

No comment had been his catchphrase ever since he had returned to London a day and a half ago.

No comment to the reporters eager to get a scoop. *No comment* to his employees, who had backed away as soon as they had recognised the warning intent in his eyes should they choose to pursue their curiosity.

Thus far, he had fielded three phone calls from an excitable Izzy, demanding to know what was going on and asking when the big day was going to be, because she would have to start shopping for a hat. He had done his best to quell her ridiculous enthusiasm but for once he was discovering that there were situations in life he could not readily cope with.

He impatiently pushed himself back from the desk and swivelled the chair to stare out of the window. For once, his door was closed. No one dared knock on it. He had been like a bear with a sore head and they all knew better than to disturb him.

Ellie.

He'd texted her. Obviously, that had been perfectly reasonable, because he had to know when 'no comment' could morph into 'things didn't work out as expected'. Today's hot-off-the press news would, he knew, be history within days, but still, he needed to know how to play things out, and he had given his word to her that he would wait until she was comfortable telling her mother the truth.

She'd replied to his embarrassingly long-winded text quite simply.

All's fine here, thanks. Will keep you in the loop. I will tell Mum it's off by the end of next week.

He'd be in Hawaii by then.

He would be facing curious family members and he would not be able to shut himself inside an office, having pinned a metaphorical *Enter at your own risk* sign on the door.

He would…

What would he do? Say? *Think?*

For a few seconds he was swamped by a suffocating sensation of powerlessness. It was like a blanket over him, stifling his ability to think straight. All he could see in his mind's eye was Ellie, with her smooth, calm face, her intelligent grey eyes and, behind that calm intelligence, all that fiery, sexy passion that had energised him a way he would never have imagined possible.

Walking away had made sense, but for once doing what *made sense* had not worked in his favour. Because, if anything, she was in his head more than she had ever been.

Why? He was conditioned to run the minute things started getting heavy with a woman. So why was he dragging his heels now? Especially when Ellie had been the one to fire the starting gun. Was it because, for all his illusion of control, the simple truth was that he had always ambushed all chance of getting serious with anyone by choosing women he'd subconsciously known would end up boring him? Until Ellie had entered his life, leaving him here, not knowing what to do…

He frowned, absently reached for his phone, recognising that initial one-second flare of anticipation that there might be a missed call or a text waiting to be read from her, then opening up the photos he had taken in Barbados.

Yet again, he was surprised at just how many he had taken. There were pictures of her laughing, looking at him over her shoulder, sitting on the beach, making funny faces because she didn't want him pointing the lens at her, even though the provocative flare in her eyes told another story.

Suddenly suffused with restless energy, thoughts previously sluggish accelerating with astonishing speed towards conclusions that now poured out from behind carefully sealed doors, he vaulted to his feet and strode to grab the trench coat draped over the back of a chair.

Ellie heard the sound of the doorbell with a grunt of displeasure.

It was a little after nine-thirty in the evening. Her mother was asleep and she was staring at a book on her lap, masochistically enjoying the pain of replaying images of James in her head and speculating on a future that held no joy at all.

At this very moment in time, she was staring down the barrel of no job, no desire to return to London, a deadline within which the stories she had started spinning to her mother about her break-up would have to accelerate and a bottomless pit of memories that promised sleepless nights wracked with misery.

The last thing she needed was one of her mother's friends popping by to drop something off. From experience, she knew that many of her mother's friends, all of them dog owners, thought nothing of having that last dog-walk late at night, using it as an excuse to deliver something or other, or nip in for a cup of coffee and a quick chat.

She opened the door with her polite expression at the ready…and for a few electrifying seconds felt the blood drain from her face as she stared up at the last person she expected to see standing outside her mother's house.

A feeling of *déjà vu* slammed into her with the force of a sledgehammer and it was all she could do to remain standing in the doorway, as rigid as a block of marble.

What the heck was *he* doing here?

How many times did he have to walk away before he realised that *walking away* should remove the option of suddenly materialising on her doorstep?

She thought back to their last conversation, to her admission that she had fallen in love with him… She'd never seen a guy back away so fast. He'd seen the conflagration ahead, and had run in the opposite direction just as fast as his legs could take him. Even though she'd expected nothing less, she'd still been devastated at his response.

Mortification surged through her, as well as mounting anger. 'What do you want?' she demanded bluntly. 'What are you doing here?'

'Let me in.'

'Over my dead body.' But she couldn't help but sneak a glance towards the staircase behind her, because if her mother ventured out of her bedroom getting rid of James would not be possible.

Yes, Ellie had begun the process of cementing all the differences between her and James. All those niggling things that were already bricks in the wall that would eventually separate them.

With a timeline set for herself of a mere week, she knew the process would have to be ratcheted up. But at this point in time, a mere couple of days since James had returned to London, the foundations she had begun to lay would be blown out of the water should her mother clap eyes on the guy shamelessly standing at the front door.

She was infuriated that, despite everything she was feeling, she could still tune into his over-the-top sexuality with such effortless ease. The guy had practically had a seizure when she had admitted her true feelings for him, yet here she was, *still* fighting to ward off the spool of vibrant images unravelling in her head.

'Where is your mother?'

'Asleep,' Ellie said sharply. 'And I don't want you coming in because I don't want her to know that you're here.'

She loved him.

She'd closed her eyes, gritted her teeth and admitted how she felt, because that was the sort of person she was. Honest, upfront and straightforward. But what had he done? He'd run faster than a sprinter at the sound of the starting gun.

Now, with her foot poised to nudge the door shut in his face, he felt a sickening sense of panic that he might have left things too late, because the truth was that love when it fell on barren ground, was quick to turn to hate…

What would he do without her in his life?

He felt giddy at the flashbacks that poured into his head—watching her down-bent head as she fiddled on her iPad, searching for just the thing he had asked for, her calm amusement at all his rowdy employees, who always seemed to do as she asked whenever she asked, the way she had guarded her private life and then shared it with him, handing him the gift of her confidences…

'I was a complete fool.' There was no point trying to preserve his dignity or play games in which he might emerge the winner. There was just this moment in time and his one chance to try and fix what he had wilfully broken.

'I don't want to have this conversation. I want you to go before Mum hears someone at the door. She might be a sound sleeper, but doorbells can wake people up. I don't want her seeing you. You're not getting it, James. *Don't just stand there staring at me!*'

'I'm getting that you opened your heart to me and I—'

'Now I *really* want you to go!' The last thing Ellie needed to hear was a minute-by-minute recap of her soul-baring confession. When she had admitted to him how she felt, she hadn't expected to clap eyes on him again, but now he was here, larger than life, and it was agony.

'You love me.' He breathed urgently, his voice lacking its usual self-assurance. 'And it's mutual.' He said that very fast, to forestall her slamming the door on him.

On the verge of shutting the door very firmly on his well-heeled loafer, Ellie paused and looked at him suspiciously.

She'd been down this road before, hadn't she? *Let's carry on*, he'd urged. *Where's the harm? Let's get what we have out of our systems and then we can break up...why not?*

But surely he wouldn't be so cruel as to use

her own declaration of love against her in some stupid quest to take what he still wanted? Did he think that her loving him made her a dead cert for a replay, using the same reasoning he had used before? Was he arrogant enough to think that he would be doing her a favour by inviting her back into his bed, and would use whatever verbal tools he wanted, knowing that she was vulnerable to them all?

'I hate you,' she whispered, already in full defence mode at her own internal line of reasoning. It had leap frogged from assumption to assumption until she had managed to convince herself that she could not possibly believe anything he had come to say. Least of all some crazy, mumbled admission of love which he had pulled out of a hat like the proverbial rabbit.

She heard the shuffle of footsteps overhead and stifled a groan of frustration.

'Just go! Mum's waking up…'

'Let me in. She doesn't have to know that I'm here. I want to talk to you. When I'm done talking, I'll leave and she will never know that I've been in the first place.'

'Ellie? Did the doorbell just ring?'

Her mother's thin voice quavered from the bedroom door which was just up the narrow stairs and mercifully out of sight.

'Get in,' she snapped at James, channelling

him past her and towards the sitting room, into which he obediently vanished, leaving her to take the stairs two at a time, just preventing her mother from trundling down to see what the fuss was all about.

Five minutes later, she was in the sitting room, door closed, heart beating so fast she felt it was going to burst right out of her chest. She didn't know what he was there for. He'd mentioned something about love, but it was clear and always had been that he hadn't the faintest idea what *love* was.

The bottom line was that she had settled her mother back to bed after mumbling vaguely that nothing was happening, there was no need to come down—*nothing to see here*. But her mother's eyes had been curious, and Ellie would have to dispatch James before curiosity got the better of sleep. Because, if her mother decided to see for herself what was going on, then all the hard work she had done building up stories of incompatibility, would have been for nothing.

In her mother's mind, the very essence of *love* would be a guy racing hundreds of miles to be with the person he loved because he couldn't bear to be apart from her.

She remained by the closed door, leaning against it, arms folded and eyes narrowed as she looked at him for a few seconds in stony, unforgiving silence.

'Speak, and make it quick, James. I don't want Mum coming downstairs and finding you sitting here.'

'I can't say what I've come here to say with you standing there by the door, like a prison warden waiting to escort a criminal from the building.'

Ellie sourly interpreted that to mean that he wanted her close, close enough to reach out and touch her. If he had come here hoping to scratch an itch that hadn't conveniently disappeared as he'd hoped, then he would surely suspect that one touch and she'd be right back in his arms?

After all, she loved him, and love made idiots of everyone. Look at poor, deluded Naomi!

For the sake of voices not being heard, because noise had an irritating habit of travelling to all sorts of nooks and crannies in the small cottage, she edged closer. But, instead of perching on the sofa next to him, she adopted a stiff position on one of the chairs, from which she continued to look at him with jaundiced suspicion. It was an effort to keep memories at bay. She could feel them just there, waiting to surge forward to undermine all her barely-there resistance.

'I've begun to explain things to Mum,' she

burst out fiercely, leaning forward. 'I've begun to tell her that we're very different people, too different for things to work out between us. I've begun to let her down, and it's not *fair* of you to just show up here so you can ruin *everything*.'

'We're barely engaged. How can our differences be rising to the surface so fast?'

'I *know* you!' Bright patches of colour scored her cheeks. 'Of course you were never going to fall in love with me. Do you think I haven't seen the way you are with all those women you dated in the past?' She looked away and her voice was low, bitter and honest. 'No matter what they looked like, when it comes to women there's only so much you're capable of giving, and all of it can be summed up in two words. *Good sex*.'

'Just *good*?'

'I'm glad you think this is funny,' Ellie said sharply.

'I don't.' He raked his fingers through his hair and leant forward, arms resting loosely on his thighs.

'I'm not climbing back into bed with you, and if I was stupid enough to fall for you then I'm also smart enough to know how the ground lies.'

James gazed at the mutinous set of her mouth, the defiant glitter in her eyes, and marvelled that he hadn't recognised what he felt for her sooner than he had. Surely he should have clocked that so much more had pulled him to her than some passing attraction?

She fired him up on every front. She was demanding, smart and had spent three years making him adapt to her without him really realising it. It was crazy that he hadn't seen that for what it was—a slow drift to an emotion he only now recognised and accepted.

'I don't want you falling back into bed with me,' he countered softly, and a shadow of bewilderment flashed across her features for a barely perceptible second or two.

He winced, thinking that those were the tramlines her thoughts were travelling down—that the only thing he could possibly have come for was sex. He honestly couldn't blame her.

'Good!' Ellie said stiffly. 'Because there's no way I intend to do that.'

'I wouldn't ask you to, unless there was a ring on your finger.'

'I beg your pardon?'

'I love you.'

Ellie stared. Her mouth fell open. Her brain moved back sluggishly half an hour, to recall his opening words when she had greeted him at the front door.

Had he meant what he'd said? *That he loved her?*

'I don't understand...' She managed to breathe

while her heart picked up frantic speed and her mouth dried up so that she could barely swallow. Joined up thinking was proving difficult.

'When we went to Barbados…' He sighed heavily, channelling his thoughts. 'Falling into bed with you… I didn't look beyond a straightforward situation of two people who had discovered their mutual attraction to one another, recognised it and decided to follow where it led. Under a tropical sun, things blossomed, and it was all very black and white.

'I look back on my life and I see that it was always very black and white when it came to relationships. I knew what loss was about, and in my mind it was always associated with the emotional freefall that came from loving someone and then being let down by them. If you never loved, then you could never be let down.'

'And what began in Barbados was going to stay in Barbados,' Ellie said softly, remembering just how clear he had been on the rules of the game, at which point she had blithely deferred thinking about tomorrow because today was too much fun.

'Come and sit next to me,' he murmured, patting the space beside him on the sofa. Ellie hesitantly shifted over to the spot and curled up, feet tucked underneath her, still too suspicious to go too close but already opening up to the roughened honesty of his voice and what he was saying to her.

He covered her hand with his but respected the small distance she had made to maintain between them.

'That was the plan,' he said gravely.

'Until Naomi appeared and blew everything out of the water.'

'Everything had been blown out of the water long before then,' he mused thoughtfully. 'I always assumed that I was immune to emotional involvement with any woman. Like I said, I lost both lost parents when I was young, but you lost a parent devoted to you. I lost parents who were devoted to one another. Money bought them freedom from any kind of conscience. They dipped in and out of our lives. They were spectators, you could say, although in Izzy's case perhaps that would be an exaggeration. She got the brunt of their attention. For me…'

He shook his head ruefully. 'Not so much. You'd think, that being the case, that their loss would have been felt less, but not so. It felt like questions I had yet to ask could then never be answered.'

Ellie shifted closer to him so that her knee was touching his thigh and she could feel the spread of warmth from his body, enfolding her like a safety blanket.

It struck her that there was something about him that had always made her feel safe, even when she had just been his dutiful secretary. She had always known that he had her back. When she thought about it, all the time he'd been *telling* her that he didn't do emotional investment, he had been *showing* her that he did. And that had culminated in him trekking across the Atlantic to hold her hand and support her because he had known that she would need him, even without her having to tell him. He *knew* her, just as she knew him.

'I had an ill-fated relationship shortly after the death of our parents,' he admitted heavily. 'I would say that that was the nail in the coffin of any inclination I might have had to test the waters of emotional involvement.'

'What happened?'

'I sought refuge in the wrong woman. I was lost, and I foolishly thought that I needed someone to help me find my way. It was a learning curve. After that, I closed myself off, and I liked it that way. I liked knowing that I was in control of everything and everyone. No unpleasant surprises. Women came and went and there was no attachment. If any of them started thinking outside the box, well, I guess, looking back, I was pretty ruthless, but it was a ruthlessness I never questioned.'

Mesmerised by this outpouring of heartfelt admissions, Ellie could only stare at him, round-eyed.

'I always knew the score, so when we became lovers I assumed you did as well, because you knew me as well as I knew myself. No attachments. Three years working with someone…' He smiled wryly. 'You were all but my wife without the ring on your finger.'

'That's hardly true.' Ellie flushed and lowered her eyes.

'Maybe not then but certainly once we became lovers.' He stared broodingly at her, then smiled again—a lazy, rueful smile that sent a tingle racing through her. 'I'd never felt so comfortable with anyone before. Of course, now I know why. I was in love with you, and everything was different. The lights had been switched on, only I didn't realise it. I just knew that I wasn't ready for things between us to end.'

'And yet when I…when I told you how I felt…'

'I did what I was programmed to do,' he admitted ruefully. 'I fled, but there was only so far I could run and for only so long. The last day and a half have been hell, and there was no way I could contemplate going to Hawaii and pretending that my life wasn't in freefall without you in it.'

Every word he said was music to her ears. She had bared her soul and now he was baring his.

'So,' he concluded, reaching towards her to tangle his fingers in her hair, eyes pinned to her face. 'I can't live without you. I love you and I need you and I was a fool for not recognising the symptoms of love sooner. I told you that I wouldn't expect you to sleep with me without a ring on your finger…so, will you marry me?'

'I think…' Ellie smiled and looked at him with all the love she was now free to express. 'I think you know the answer to that…'

Ellie slipped her hand into James's, looked up at him and smiled.

She couldn't have been happier. Yet now, a mere couple of days after his proposal, she found that she was nervous as they walked towards the private function room in the five-star hotel where she would meet his assembled family.

'You look radiant,' he murmured, tipping her chin so that their eyes met. 'And it's not as though congratulations haven't already been flying across the airwaves.' He grinned. 'Izzy has texted a hundred times. They can't wait to get to know you.'

Ellie glanced down at her dress, jade-green and softly falling from thin spaghetti straps to just above her knees. She had angsted over what to wear and, concluded, with precious little time to choose, that the outfit would be fine for a lunchtime do, bearing in mind that many more would be joining them for an early supper—including, she had gathered, Max's fiancée Mia's sprawling family. She took a deep breath and met his reassuring grin with a smile.

'Seems unfair that Max and Mia's big day is just round the corner and we've gate-crashed it with an announcement of our engagement…'

'We didn't do that,' James pointed out. 'A certain malevolent ex did…'

He thought back to the text he had received from Naomi a couple of days ago. She hadn't been able to resist getting in touch so that she could rub his nose in it, pleased with herself for landing him in a place she'd figured he'd loathe. It had given him huge satisfaction to inform her of the aisle he would be walking down with the woman he loved right there by his side. No need to block her number, because he knew that he wouldn't be hearing from her again any time soon.

'Besides,' he added thoughtfully, 'I think Max is only too pleased that he's not the only die-hard bachelor to find himself hopelessly in love. I spoke to him just before we flew, and he actually crowed that yet again big brother is leading the way…'

'You always manage to say the right things,' Ellie murmured, and raised her eyebrows when he replied without batting an eyelid,

'Is that the sound of you admitting that you'll be marrying the perfect man?' He burst out laughing, pushing open the imposing door in front of them at the same time, 'No…don't answer that. Your expression speaks louder than words and, my darling, I wouldn't have it any other way. Now…time to brave the lion's den…'

Ellie had no time for her nerves to flourish. They opened the door to a quiet gathering. Max and Mia, and Izzy and her fiancé Gabriel, and a little child with long, dark hair and bright, curious eyes.

The room had been adorned with flair, a picture-book story of everything Hawaii had to offer. Beautiful plants dotted the huge space and stunning local paintings adorned the walls. Ellie took it all in and smiled, relaxing as the women leapt to their feet and came towards her while James, smiling, moved to kiss his sister in passing before joining the guys.

A quiet segregation of the sexes, soon to be remedied, but just for the moment Ellie was enfolded by Izzy and Mia, with Rosa bobbing around and clamouring to join the club, just the thing to set her at ease.

'I can't believe James is getting married!' Izzy

squealed. 'Mind you, the real shock was Max.' She hugged Mia, a striking olive-skinned girl with skin as smooth as satin and long, brown hair pinned to one side with a deep red hibiscus flower, and kept her arm slung affectionately round the other woman's shoulders. They both looked at Ellie, eyes lively and warm.

'We girls have to tame these guys,' Mia confided, grinning. 'And that includes Gabriel!'

'Can I tame someone?' Rosa demanded, which was the cue for the guys to burst out laughing as Max asked what plots were being concocted. And then Ellie was being shepherded to the table, where champagne was waiting to be drunk and a mouth-watering array of local dishes were set out, with two waiters standing stiffly by the doors, ready to be summoned to serve the food and pour the drinks.

In one sweeping glance, she took them all in—her new family. She was barely aware of champagne corks popping but she *was* aware of glasses being raised for a toast to Max and Mia.

'To Max and Mia!' she said on cue.

Her turn would soon be coming and she couldn't wait…

* * * * *